EDGE

EDGE

Diane Tullson

Stoddart Kids

TORONTO • NEW YORK

Published in Canada in 2002 by
Stoddart Kids, a division of
Stoddart Publishing Co. Limited
895 Don Mills Road, 400-2 Park Centre, Toronto, Ontario M3C 1W3

Published in the United States in 2002 by
Stoddart Kids, a division of
Stoddart Publishing Co. Limited
PMB 128, 4500 Witmer Estates, Niagara Falls, New York 14305-1386

www.stoddartkids.com

To order Stoddart books please contact General Distribution Services
In Canada Tel. (416) 213-1919 Fax (416) 213-1917
Email cservice@genpub.com
In the United States Toll-free tel. 1-800-805-1083 Toll-free fax 1-800-481-6207
Email gdsinc@genpub.com

06 05 04 03 02 1 2 3 4 5

National Library of Canada Cataloguing in Publication Data

Tullson, Diane, 1958–
Edge

ISBN 0-7737-6230-2

I. Title.

PS8589.U6055E3 2002   jC813'.6   C2002-900840-9
PZ7.T7852Ed 2002

Cover and text design: Tannice Goddard
Cover illustration: Silvia Pecota

*We acknowledge for their financial support of our publishing program the Canada Council,
the Ontario Arts Council, and the Government of Canada through the
Book Publishing Industry Development Program (BPIDP).*

Printed and bound in Canada

For Wayne

ACKNOWLEDGEMENTS

Thanks to the writers of Pen & Inklings, Delta, British Columbia, for their incisive reading of the manuscript, especially Shelley Hrdlitschka, who saw it as a book before I did.

CHAPTER ONE

—m—

"I wonder what Mom would bury me in." I pull my heels up on the rung of the stool and watch as Chuck combs out a silver-haired lady with fine bones, deep in the sleep of death. His hand pauses on the comb.

Chuck Mann is an undertaker. He and his brother, Sid, run Mann's Funeral Home. Chuck drives a big black car with a license plate that says "DIGGER." He uses a cushion to see over the wheel — I've been taller than him for a couple of years already.

My mother works with Chuck. My mom is a funeral singer.

"Not that awful dress I got for Cousin Myron's wedding. Don't let her bury me in that."

Chuck sprays the curls lightly and sets them around the dead woman's face. "The white one? I thought you looked like a princess in that dress."

"I looked like larvae."

"Larvae in the casket. That could have a nasty impact on business."

He takes a photo from his work stand and holds it next

to the woman, making minute adjustments of the curls. It's a picture of the woman with a man, taken awhile ago judging from their clothes. In the photo her hair is almost blue. I point this out to Chuck.

"The 'blue rinse' ladies. That's what we used to call them, the ones that went every week to the beauty parlor." He strokes a strand of hair from the woman's forehead. "This lady hasn't seen a beauty parlor in a long time."

"How can you tell?"

"Marks from the bed, you know. She's been in hospital for years."

The woman's silver curls catch the light.

"She's beautiful."

Chuck sets the photo back on his work stand. "Yes. She is."

"Is that her husband in the picture?"

"Probably. Or a brother. He must be gone, though. This lady is ninety-two."

I imagine the steel-eyed man in the photo looking down at us. Waving. I straighten the collar on the woman's blouse. It feels like old satin, nice and thick.

"I'd like to be buried in something black."

Chuck turns to the side, his lab coat stretched over his round belly. "Black? I never wear it. It makes me look underfed." He sucks in his cheeks like a fashion model.

"An undertaker who won't wear black. How do you expect to scare little kids?"

Chuck arranges the woman on her pillow so that her curls don't crush, then he wheels her off to the side of the room. I blow a kiss to the old guy in the photo.

Chuck strips off his gloves and washes his hands. "I'll

tell you what's scary. That blue eye shadow you're wearing."

He pulls over a cart with stacked trays of little bottles and tubes. Tidy bins hold lipsticks, brushes, pencils, liners, and mascara. He studies my eyes. "A makeup brush in the wrong hands is a dangerous weapon." He swivels me around on the stool. "May I?"

I nod. He dampens a clean cotton pad and smooths it over my face.

"Ooh, Marlie, you're nice and warm."

"Nice and alive, you mean."

"And no zits. How many fourteen year olds can brag about that?"

"Mouse-brown hair but, hey, I've got great skin."

"Yup, you're an unblemished canvas. Just that one small wart."

"Chuck!"

"I'm kidding." He pulls out a tube of pinky-brown and squirts some on a swab stick.

"It looks like melted milkshake."

"Have faith, my girl. I am a master."

It's true. Chuck's clients always look better than their pictures. I close my eyes.

"So, you're not thinking about leaving this earthly world, are you? Planning your funeral and all that?" There's a tinge of concern in Chuck's voice. "You're settling in okay?" he says. "Finding your way around the school? Starting high school can be tough, with all the new kids."

I'm glad my eyes are closed. It's easier to lie. "I'm fine. I was just making conversation."

Chuck's hands feel like feathers, light and sure. "Because you could talk to me if anything was bothering you. You know that, right?"

"Uh-huh." I blink my eyes open. I like that he thinks I could. He makes it seem like I'm in control.

"Close your eyes. I want to use a little powder on your brows. Makeup is illusion and illusion is good. But the edges, Marlie, must disappear." Chuck takes on a French accent. "You blend away zee artist's hand so all zat is zeen is zee skin. Blend, blend, blend. Dere." He hands me a small mirror. "Have a look."

I hold the mirror and whistle softly. "You're good."

Too bad he can't do something about the hair.

"What's that stink?" The girl's voice behind me in the crowded school hall raises the hair on my arms. Loren Miller. And one of her hordes. The smell of Wednesday's special at the school cafeteria is wafting in the corridor, but I know that's not what she means. "Oh, it's just MARLENA. I thought it was something dead." An elbow jabs me right between the shoulder blades. They're laughing.

I suck in a breath. Don't run. Just breathe normally. They'll go, sooner or later.

"You're in our way." A shoulder slams me into a locker. "Some of us have places to go." Another slam. This time my face smacks the painted green metal. More laughter. "You're clumsy, girl. You should take something for that."

The hallway is full of people, everybody heading for lunch. Some eyes slide over me, but mostly no one notices. No one sees a thing. Loren throws a sneer over her shoulder like salt.

I slip into the quiet of the library. To my invisible world.

Ms. Grimshaw, the librarian, glances up when I come in. "Marlie, there are books in the mending box that need attention. I'll leave that with you today." Her black hair is pulled back really tight, so her white-pale eyes bug out like a reptile's. I've seen her fix those eyes on some poor tenth grader and just about make him cry. They bore into your soul, those eyes do. She's wearing one of her long dark skirts and a dark sweater with the sleeves pushed up. I saw her come into the library once with a brightly colored scarf. But as soon as she'd taken off her coat, she snatched it into a sleeve.

I've been Ms. Grimshaw's slave for a couple of months, since the beginning of school. It's a small price for the safe haven of the library. In my personal war zone of James Last Secondary School, the library is Switzerland. Neutral. Boring. No one ever comes here, certainly not Loren Miller. It's perfect. If I have to be alone, the library is a good place to be. Ms. Grimshaw gives me what approximates a smile then bustles out. I wonder what she has in her lunch bag. Something webbed, maybe.

"Oh, and before I forget." Ms. Grimshaw has turned in the doorway. I wipe the guilty thoughts from my mind. "There's a book on my desk. I wonder if you'd read it and let me know what you think?"

She's gone before I can answer. I pull my lunch from my pack and go over to the window to eat.

It's better than television. There are the boys, like always, playing basketball, the usual clumps of girls roving, and the smoke pit where the degenerates hang out. There's Keely Willson, my ex-best friend, looking like everyone is watching her.

I can see the edge of the parking lot, where the senior guys lean on their cars and drink enormous Cokes.

And I can see the elementary school, just down the hill. Its fields are crawling with kids. I try to pick out my younger brother, Elliott, in the schoolyard. It's not easy, him being so small. If I see him at all it's probably my imagination.

Elliott is seven. He has golden-brown hair that he combs straight forward and eyes that change color from gray to green. I've seen my mother watching him, her eyes getting all soft and doe-like. I know she'd like to pick him up and hold him, if she thought no one would see her. I would too.

I finish my lunch as I do the mending, then head to the little glassed-in alcove behind the circulation desk where Ms. Grimshaw has her office. It's a tightly packed catacomb of new and old books, crates and bins, ancient video equipment, and a coat rack where Ms. Grimshaw keeps her dark-colored coat. A flowery smell hangs over everything. It smells like Ms. Grimshaw. I grab the one book that isn't part of a tidy stack on her desk and go back to the window.

Maybe I got the wrong one. It's one of her own books. The same flowery smell comes off the pages like breath. Someone has written in the front of it: "An antidote for the isolated life. With my enduring love, C."

Opening that book is like looking in someone's underwear drawer. The very thought of Ms. Grimshaw having an "enduring love" borders on the bizarre. Maybe he buys her the colorful scarves that she wears to please him then hides in her coat sleeve.

The type is small, the kind that makes you yawn to read it. On some pages, in the margins, are tightly written notes in blue ink. There are question marks after a few of the notes, and she's marked some passages with a daisy-like star. I close the book.

I open it again, to the inscription. "The isolated life." Apparently Ms. Grimshaw has made her assessment and has filed me under the Ls for lonely. Or loser.

From the window I look for Keely on the schoolyard. She's easy to spot, in her bright blue volleyball suit. There are four girls with her wearing these suits. She's laughing and they are, too.

The bell is going to go. I toss the book into my pack. I want to be out of here before Ms. Grimshaw comes back. Ms. Grimshaw with the enduring love. Be still my pounding heart.

The bell at the elementary school has just rung, and little kids are funneling into the school like ants. Every day, it's the same thing. The elementary kids go back in and the crows come down off the roof to ravage dropped wrappers for crumbs of granola bars and potato chips. I've seen the crows line up on the edge of the school roof, maybe fifty of them, like they know the bell is going to ring. When the kids start running for the doors, the crows take wing, like a black umbrella over the yard. Today, it's weird — there's not a crow in sight. Maybe that's why I don't look for Elliott, like I always do. Because maybe I already know he isn't there.

CHAPTER TWO

—͢ⁿⁿ͢—

"MARLENA PETERS TO THE OFFICE," the voice barks from the classroom speaker.

"Hey, MARLENA, what did you do? Put a library book back in the wrong spot?" It's a group of girls in short skirts and they're laughing. They must be friends of Loren's. I pretend that I don't hear them. From the other side of the room someone lets out a soft snort. I clear my desk in a hurry.

The principal, Mrs. Birk, is sitting behind an enormous polished desk, reading from a manila file. She closes it when I come in and looks me over. Her inspection pauses on my sweatshirt, and I glance down to see crumbs from my lunch. Without smiling, she motions for me to sit down. She holds her hand out straight for a moment, checking her careful manicure. Her nails gleam a deep red. When she speaks, her voice is clipped and precise, a "let's get down to business" voice.

"Marlena, your brother, Elliott, did not report to class after lunch. His school is asking if you know the reason."

Elliott. My stomach lurches. I swallow hard.

Mrs. Birk leans forward. On the corner of her eyeglasses is a designer logo. Her hair looks like it was parted with a razor.

"It's Marlie."

Mrs. Birk sucks a breath through her teeth. "Well, then, Marlie." Her eyebrows lift above her glasses when she says this. "The school has talked to your mother. What can you add to this?"

Now my mouth is dry, with the little bit of spit forming shards in the back of my throat. A tidy stack of pink phone messages is impaled on a spike at Mrs. Birk's crisp left cuff. She's looking in the file again, then she looks at me. "Well?"

I shrug. My face is burning. "I don't know."

Mrs. Birk sits back with a sigh. "Your parents have been divorced for two years now, is that right?"

I nod. My head is starting to pound.

"And your father? He's not been well?"

She's holding that file open in front of her, like it's some holy tome. Her red nails glare against the pale-colored folder.

I shrug again. "He has this depression thing. It's just low level."

"Well, I'm sure there is no cause for concern." She claps the file closed. "Why don't you go back up to class?" Her mouth straightens into a quick smile, then resumes its clench. "I'll call you if you're needed further."

Mrs. Birk reaches for the pink messages, already focused on something else. Her bright nails make a tapping noise on the desk.

I want to scream at her. Elliott is gone. It doesn't matter

why. He's not here, he's missing, and he's gone. I stand up and pain rings my head like a helmet.

Mrs. Birk picks up the phone and punches in a number with the eraser end of her pencil. I blink, because the pencil is wavering in front of my eyes. My mouth fills with spit and my stomach cramps.

My mind registers what's going to happen, but my feet won't move, and there's no time.

I hurl.

All over Mrs. Birk's nice shiny desk.

"Oh!" she shrieks. "Oh!"

A puddle of Doritos and tuna fish creeps toward the message spike.

"Oh!" She pushes away from the desk, her knees clamped together like that's going to somehow contain the flow. Her red fingernails curl over her chest. "Mrs. Orthney!" she cries. "Mrs. Orthney!"

The secretary comes running.

If Mrs. Birk had kids, she'd have a picture of them on her desk, two shining faces of two perfect children, children who would get straight As and play rep soccer and go to everyone's birthday parties. Mrs. Birk's parking spot wouldn't hold a sporty BMW, but a minivan, with a bumper sticker that would read, "Proud Parent of a St. Margaret's Honor Student." No, clearly, before today, Mrs. Birk had never been hurled on.

Wiping my mouth on the sleeve of my sweatshirt, I flee.

I slam out of the school door, the steps a blur, the school flag snapping like a whip at my back. I head for the elementary school down the hill.

I'm feeling way better now. I take big gulps of fresh air

and spell "expedition" to stop from crying. I force myself to walk.

"Hey." The voice makes me jump. It's a girl, sitting in the back of a blue pickup truck. She's wearing a black denim jacket with the collar turned up against the autumn cold. A black cap shadows her eyes.

"I saw it all. You shouldn't let them get away with it."

I think about Elliott. And crows. "You saw what?"

The girl flips a Coke can from the back of the truck and it clatters on the pavement. "Loren, 'The Terminator.' I saw her rough you up in the hall."

"Oh, that." Thinking about Loren makes my stomach roll again. "No, I'm not leaving because of her. It's my brother. Some trouble with my brother."

The girl waves her hand, like she's brushing me off. A deep blue tattoo covers her knuckles. "Whatever."

Dismissed, I head back down the sidewalk.

"Hey." Her voice stops me. I glance back, her cap just visible over the side of the truck.

"Someone always sees."

I turn again to go, but her words stay with me. Like a threat.

❖ ❖ ❖

Two police cars are pulled up at the elementary school and Chuck's car, too. They're all in the office. Chuck's not wearing his lab coat, and the buttons on his shirt are straining. His pants are a strange orange color, like he washed them with something that ran. He sees me and takes my hand.

"It looks like it was your dad. The cops are just in with McLean now."

McLean lives next door. He's Keely's brother and Elliott's best friend. He hasn't said more than two words to me, ever. He talks to Elliott. I've heard them in Elliott's room yattering and chattering. Who knows about what.

"Your mom, she's pretty worked up over this." Chuck is talking quietly. "She's mad and she's scared."

I look over his shoulder at my mother. She's wearing her navy blue suit, from work, the sleeves rumpled from where she's had her arms crossed. A strand of dark hair has escaped her careful knot and her green eyes are rimmed with red. She's pacing, her slim shoulders hunched, clutching Elliott's school picture in one hand, a box of tissues in the other. She doesn't look over at me.

"This is scary for everyone, Marlie." I smile at him and he squeezes my hand. Up until a couple of years ago, Chuck and Dad were best friends. Then there was the divorce. But even before the divorce, Chuck was more of a father for Elliott and me. I don't know what I would do without him.

The principal's office door opens, and a police officer nods at my mother. "The boy says it was Elliott's father. Apparently he was waiting at the schoolyard fence when the boys went out at lunchtime. Elliott left with him in his car."

"Oh, thank God," my mother says. Then, "That son of a . . ." She looks at me and stops. Her face is red and blotchy and her lips stretch into a thin line.

When Elliott was a baby, the very first time he smiled, it was for me. I used to get up with Mom to give him his bottle. It would still be dark out, maybe five in the morning. At first Mom didn't like it, said I'd be too tired at school. She'd change him, and warm up the bottle in the microwave, then doze in the rocker while I fed Elliott in my lap on the floor. Before he got too sleepy again I'd bounce him on my knee and sing funny songs to him. I made faces and he'd try to do the same thing. Around six Mom would rouse herself and put Elliott back down. I'd go back to bed, too. I wished I could sleep with him, in his crib. He smelled so sweet.

Sometimes, when I was drifting back to sleep, I'd hear my mom and dad.

"Brad, you don't want to be late again."

"I've got lots of time. Just ten more minutes."

"No, you don't. You have to leave in half an hour."

"I'll skip breakfast."

"You can't lose this job, Brad. You just can't."

Then it would get quiet, and Mom would cry, and when I went to school, Dad's door would still be closed and Mom would be sitting at the table with an empty pot of coffee, staring blankly at the newspaper.

The police officer is asking Mom questions now. "Where is he likely to go? Does he have family anywhere? How much money does he have?"

Chuck interrupts to say, "If you need us, we'll be outside." The police officer waves us off. Chuck leads me out to the playground. The air smells like it always does at the playground, that sweet, fresh smell of freedom. My throat is closing tight.

Chuck keeps looking at me, like he wants to say something. Like, he's sorry. But he doesn't. Instead he says, "How about a swing?"

Chuck is positioning himself in the black rubber seat.

"I don't think so."

"C'mon. I haven't had a swing in years."

That's obvious. He's testing the chains, looking up at the frame, gauging its strength. Tentatively, he gives himself a little push. His butt in the swing looks like a great pinched pumpkin. His round legs are knock-kneed because of the way the seat is squeezing him. His face is red and shiny and as the swing carries him down, sweeping past me, he tries to smile. But tears are running down his cheeks.

CHAPTER THREE

—⌇⌇⌇—

Elliott should have known better. He has blinders on when it comes to Dad. It's because Dad plays video games with him. The two of them will hook up their handhelds and play like all the world turns on getting past level four. Mostly I sit there looking at the social worker. She's there to supervise, and tries to be unobtrusive. It never works.

Before the first time Dad took us, a year and a half ago, we'd spend weekends at his apartment. In the parking lot of his building is a basketball net and we'd shoot hoops all Saturday afternoon, Elliott and me against Dad. On Sundays we'd take the train downtown to the huge library, get an armful of books, then eat pizza by the slice in the park.

Even the first time it happened, I knew it was wrong. But we'd had this great weekend, and we were going for ice cream, which we always did on the way home, and Dad said, "Come on, we'll go for a Sunday drive." Dad was pumped. He was so happy. We stopped for burgers just before the border and I woke up at dawn parked on the side of the road, Dad snoring behind the wheel. My teeth felt fuzzy and my neck was stiff from sleeping in the car. All I could think of was Mom, and what she was feeling right then, and how she must be worried half to death. Maybe Dad thought about it, too, because he took us back that night.

If Dad thought Mom would understand, even a little, he was wrong. Him taking us changed everything, for Elliott and me, for Dad, for Mom. But mostly for Mom. I don't think Mom ever thought about us without thinking about it happening again.

❖ ❖ ❖

Locker doors are banging on both sides of me as students grab what they need for morning classes. I'm tossing my lunch bag into my locker when an arm snakes over my shoulder, and before the hand clamps over my eyes, I get an image of glaring white skin — skin like someone in Chuck's workroom — and the smell of underarms.

"Guess who." It's not a question. It's the voice from the truck.

"Black jacket, pickup truck. Now could you get your hand off my face?"

The hand releases. I recognize the tattoo as it slithers back to its owner.

"Ravin." She's standing really close to me. "Ravin with an 'i.'" She's wearing a black T-shirt and jeans, and her jet-black hair is short and spiky. Her eyes are pale blue, like a husky dog's. A row of silver rings runs along one pierced eyebrow.

"Marlie."

"I know who you are." She's not smiling. Her voice has that same flat menace. "I heard what you did to Fiona."

"Fiona?"

"Yeah, Fiona Birk, you know." She holds out her nails and flashes them, mimicking the principal. "She had to go home and change."

"Oh, no." I close my locker and lean my head against it.

"Yeah, I was in there right after you and it still stunk."

I don't know why she's telling me this. "I'm going to be late."

"Don't feel bad. You're like a hero." Ravin is leaning against the lockers, chewing a thumbnail, studying me with black-rimmed eyes. I could put my hand around her bone-white biceps and my thumb and forefinger would meet.

"Yeah, well, it's not like I meant to . . ."

Ravin cuts me off. "You," she pokes me in the arm with a stubby nail, "you don't give yourself enough credit." Then she leaves. A notebook is folded into the back pocket of her jeans. She walks like there's no one else around her. Just before the stairs, she stops and turns. The silver rings in her eyebrow glint. She doesn't smile but she nods her head.

Ravin. Ravin with an "i." Like my life isn't complicated enough.

✦ ✦ ✦

When I get home after school Mom is on the phone to someone. She's wearing jeans and an ancient sweatshirt, the same clothes she had on yesterday.

". . . well, I just thought he might have said something to you. That's all." She's pulling at the front of her hair. "I know. I know all that. Yes, I know the police talked to you. I just thought . . . yes, just call me if you hear anything." She hangs up. Her mouth has a thin, angry set to it.

"Was that Nana?" My dad's mother.

"Yes. She hasn't heard anything."

"Well, why would she?" My grandmother isn't what you'd call close to us. Mom told me that when she and Dad got married, Nana showed up to the wedding a half hour late, wearing a black dress. Nana said she thought it was navy blue. We see her maybe twice a year, and then only with Dad.

Mom sits down heavily at the table, her back to me. "I just had to try, didn't I?" Wadded-up tissues lie on the table. She takes another from a box in front of her and blows her nose. "What else is there I can do? She says Brad would never hurt him. That he's always been a good father." Her voice is muffled in tissue. "But she doesn't believe he's even sick. He's still HER little boy and he can do no wrong."

I drop my pack on the counter and empty out my books.

"Dad won't hurt Elliott." I say it quietly, more to myself. He's never even raised his voice to us.

Like she can read my mind, Mom starts talking to the tissue box again. "He used to leave Elliott in his car seat when he ran into the dry cleaners. Said he could see him from the store, that nothing was going to happen to him. I said to him, 'What happens if you get shot or have a heart attack? Who's going to know that baby is in the car?'"

Mom's fists are waving, balls of tissue in each one. "'Who's going to know he's even there?'"

I toss my lunch bag into the garbage. A lump of half-frozen hamburger oozes in the sink. I dump it into a bowl and put it in the microwave to thaw. Mom's quiet now, holding her head in her hands. I rummage in the cupboard for Hamburger Helper. Cheesy Italian. Elliott would have loved this stuff. The box shows a wholesome-looking meal, with green salad and bread sticks. We'll have ours with white Wonderbread and ketchup. The microwave beeps and I plop the meat in a pan with the noodles and sauce. Mom hasn't moved for so long I think she must be asleep. But then she says, "I'm exhausted. I'm going to bed."

She pushes back from the table and blows her nose.

"Tidy up the kitchen when you're done."

"You're not going to have some supper?" I say to her closing bedroom door.

My mom wanted to be a Nashville singer. Dad has a picture of her wearing a pale blue dress, really tight, no straps, and short. She's sitting with her legs crossed, dangling a silver high-heeled shoe from one foot. I asked her once if she still had the dress, and she laughed, "Oh, not likely. That was another life." A life before she sang at funerals. She's thirty-four. Tonight she looks closer to fifty.

I look at the pan. Noodles are congealing in an orange-colored sauce. With a sigh, I take the pan and a fork and turn on the TV.

CHAPTER FOUR

—⁓—

On Friday Ravin with an "i" shows up in the library at lunchtime, with two of her friends, a guy and a girl. The girl has a gold stud through her nostril. I wonder what happens when she sneezes. The guy is tall and thin, with short blond hair. The only other person in the library, a skinny, studious type from tenth grade, packs up quietly and leaves.

Ravin is fiddling with the laser scanner at the checkout desk, shining the red light at the other two. They laugh, but she doesn't.

I try to make my voice friendly, but in control. "You can't really be in here if you're not studying."

"Oh?" Ravin draws a scribble of red light around my face. I squeeze my eyes closed against the light.

"Yeah. Maybe you've got a paper you're working on or something?"

"A paper." Ravin looks like she's trying to remember what that is. "Nope, can't say that I do." She hoists herself lightly onto the desk and swings her legs, her heels making a *thonk thonk* sound on the side of it. She reaches over and grabs a book from the stack in front of me. From her back pocket she takes a green pen. She flips the book open and, I can hardly believe it, she's writing a number in the front of the book.

"There's a party tonight. You can come with us." She tosses the book back onto my pile and jumps off the desk. She leaves, walking in her weightless way, and the other two follow her toward the door. The girl with the nose stud glances back, kind of sizing me up.

"I know you."

I scrutinize her magenta hair, her face with its glittering nose, trying to place her.

"We were at the same elementary school. I was a year ahead of you."

"I'm sorry," I say. "I don't remember."

She smiles a half-smile and shrugs. Then they are gone.

The green ink glows on the page. I try rubbing it away with an eraser, but it just smears. So I take Ms. Grimshaw's really sharp scissors and cut the page out of the book. Then I quickly fold the page and cram it in my pocket.

✧ ✧ ✧

The crush in the hall before afternoon classes is enormous. I'm at my locker, fishing out my science text, when I hear her voice.

"Hey, I heard about Elliott."

Keely. It's Keely. My stomach does a handspring. I close my locker and turn to her. She's with three other girls. My stomach sinks.

"McLean told me. He's really bent about it. Just mopes

around his room." She turns to the girls standing with her. "My little brother is so sensitive."

One of the girls is wearing a school tracksuit, like Keely. The other two are wearing T-shirts with little logos. One is studying my shoes.

"Yeah. Thanks," I say.

"Who's Elliott?"

"Her brother." Keely answers before I can. "He's really cute. Same age as my youngest brother. They're best friends."

I sneak a quick look at Keely. She's leaning with her back on the lockers opposite mine and her eyes follow everyone who passes. "Her brother got abducted. Kidnapped, you know?"

Gasps from the T-shirt girls. "No!" Their faces fill with sympathy.

"Yeah, but . . ." I say.

"Yeah, but it was just her dad."

"Her dad?" The faces look puzzled. One looks disgusted.

"Keely!" She isn't listening to me. It's like I'm not even there.

"He did it before," she says. "Took both of you that time, didn't he?" Keely's eyes are blank. She's starting to get a zit in the middle of her chin. "But it was no big deal. I mean, he just brought you back a day late."

The T-shirt girls drift away, already bored. The other tracksuit is watching Keely. She shifts her feet a bit, and I know it's so she'll be standing just like Keely. She's got her hair in a pony. Just like Keely. She'll eat the same thing at lunch. She'll buy the same runners. She'll do anything to be just like Keely. She'll do anything for Keely. I know. I've been that girl.

I don't know when it really started, Keely not liking me. I wasn't looking for it to happen. But last spring, when we were in grade eight, Keely figured I should go out for track with her. She was doing three events, all running.

"I can't run, Keely."

"Then shot put. You'd be great at that. Your size would be a real advantage."

She made it sound like I was huge. I'm tall, but not heavy. It's just that Keely is a size three, and anyone bigger is, well, huge.

"Or discus," she added.

I could have done these events, I guess. But Loren Miller was on the track team. Loren and her horde.

"I don't think so. I pulled a muscle in my back."

"You're lying."

I laughed, thinking she was joking. She wasn't. "Why don't you just say you don't want to do it?"

"Why are you so mad? It's just track."

"It's not JUST TRACK." She exaggerated the way I said it, making her lips all loose and slobbery.

Even though Keely had never liked her, used to make jokes about her having a steel plate in her skull, she started hanging with Loren.

Then, two weeks later, after walking to school barely saying a word and ignoring me at lunch, suddenly she was friends again.

"Don't you think Matt is gorgeous?" She huddled up close to me at the lunchroom table. I could smell the soap she used, like flowers and vinegar. She was watching Matt sitting two tables over. With Leah.

"You mean Matt-and-Leah Matt?"

"Sssh." Matt and Leah had been together since the start of eighth grade. Leah was the kind of girl who never said anything mean, even when she had the chance. And Matt — he was shorter than me, but the same size as Keely. He had sandy brown hair and green eyes that grabbed you and held you and made you stop breathing.

"You're going to try for him?" I leaned in closer, excited by the conspiracy, by being with Keely again. "He'd drop Leah, if he knew you liked him. You're way better looking."

Keely smiled at me, a best-friend's smile. "You think so?"

Later, in keyboarding, I caught Matt's incredible green eyes.

"Keely likes you." That's all I said. All I had to say.

"Keely?"

"Yeah, duh."

"But me and Leah . . ."

"Whatever."

It had been a mistake to tell Matt.

"I never told her to tell him!" Keely whined. We were crowded into the washroom. Leah was sitting on the sink, sobbing. Half the girls were comforting Leah. The other half had me and Keely pinned up against the wall. "Of course, I think Matt's gorgeous," Keely said. "Everyone thinks he's gorgeous." Murmurs of assent from the girls. "But why would I say anything? I know you're going out." Keely started to cry. "I wouldn't do anything to hurt you, Leah."

It's not even like everyone believed Keely. But Loren did. So they did. Maybe even Leah did. Suddenly I was so far outside Keely and the others, pushed so far back, that I hardly existed for them.

Ravin is the first person in this school to even acknowledge I exist. Other than Loren, of course, who's always happy to remind me how much she hates me. So I hide from Loren. I hide from everyone.

Keely and the girl in the tracksuit are moving away from the lockers. "Her dad, he's a little, you know." Keely makes a swirly motion by her ear. "Anyway, Elliott will be back." She makes her way down the hall. "At least then McLean will have something to do. My little brother, he's adorable. Do you know what he did?" She's hooked up again with the T-shirts, and they're walking four abreast in the hall, their heads tilted in to one another, their shoulders touching. The other three are laughing at whatever Keely just said.

☙ ☙ ☙

"Hello?" The voice is reassuringly normal. A mother's voice.

The torn-out page from the library book is unfolded on the counter. Mom's bedroom door is closed. The house is unbearably empty.

"Is Ravin there? Please." Sweat breaks out under my arms. Maybe she isn't there. Maybe I could just hang up.

"Yes, one moment." It is such a nice normal voice. I can hear it calling, "Ravin, it's for you."

My mother never calls me Marlie. Only Marlena. "If I wanted to call you Marlie," she always says, "I would've put that on your birth certificate." Elliott is just Elliott. Maybe Ravin is just Ravin.

I hear a click and "I've got it" hollered into the mouthpiece. The mother-voice hangs up.

"Yeah."

"Ravin?"

"Yeah."

I could still hang up. It's not too late. "It's Marlie." Now it's too late.

"Give me your address. We'll be over in a while."

"Um, I was just wondering, like, what kind of party it is. What I should wear, you know?"

There's a long silence, and I think for a minute that she's hung up. Then I hear that breathy sound after someone yawns.

"Do you want to go or not?"

No. Every corpuscle, every nerve is saying no, rent a movie, clean your room, anything. I say, "Yes," and give her my address.

Then she hangs up.

I choose my newer jeans and a hooded sweatshirt. I think about putting something in my hair, some gel maybe, and trying to spike it in the front like Ravin's. Mom has emerged, and I go out to the living room where she's watching the news.

"Mom, what do you think about my hair? Does it look all right?"

Mom's eyes never leave the TV screen. It's like she thinks she'll see him there, Elliott, captured in the background of a news report. Or pulled, broken and bleeding, from some car wreck. It's like if she thinks about anything other than Elliott, he won't find his way back home. I don't think she even hears me.

I just comb my hair the way I always do.

It's 6:15. I sit by the front door to wait.

CHAPTER FIVE

———

A white minivan pulls up in the driveway, a perfectly normal minivan. Ravin is sitting in the front seat. A woman in tennis clothes is driving — nothing strange, just a mother-type woman. I climb in to the middle seat behind Ravin. The guy and girl from the library are curled up together on the back seat.

Ravin doesn't introduce me. Her mother says, "Hello, you must be Marlie. Cor, Julian, have you met Marlie?"

Cor and Julian in the back don't seem to have heard her. I open my mouth to respond, but Ravin's mother doesn't pause.

"Have you always lived here? You're not that far from us, really, just a few blocks the other side of the parkway. So you would have gone to the other elementary school? The one by the high school? You could even walk to our house, or ride your bike." The minivan slows down by some huge new-looking houses. "Is this the house? Ravin, I'll be back at ten, just after my game. You have to really swing that door to close it. Have fun!"

I watch Ravin carefully ignoring her mother. I say

thanks for the ride. Cor and Julian climb out and mumble something like "goodbye."

I've been on this street before. When Keely and I were in Girl Guides, one of the leaders lived up here and we came to her house sometimes. The Guide leader's house was brand-new. Mom said a family of four could live in the kitchen.

The party is in the garage. A patio table is set up in the middle of the floor loaded with bowls and big bottles of pop. A portable stereo on the workbench is blasting. A furnace pumps warm air through the space, and Ravin slips off her jacket. She's wearing a black tank top and I can see the poky bones of her shoulders under her pale white skin. Ravin moves among the crowd like they're her guests. There are always two or three people around her.

A group of guys are leaning on the workbench. Cor and Julian drape themselves in a corner. Some girls huddle over by the power saw. There are lawn chairs set up, but no one is sitting in them. I don't recognize anyone from my classes.

Ms. Grimshaw would like this garage. The walls are lined with plywood shelves, labeled with masking tape: camp cooler; ski boots; Xmas lights. The cardboard boxes are neatly lettered, too: Xmas lights — interior; Xmas lights — exterior; Xmas lights — spare. By the workbench is one of those boards with the little holes, with tools hanging on it, each with a black marker outline. A series of mayonnaise jars sits on the windowsill, containing screws and nails. Each of the jars is also labeled. A well-worn broom is outlined on the wall by the door.

I picture myself outlined like they do at crime scenes,

only with black marker. Whoever owns this garage would cross my arms neatly before tracing me.

I'm looking up at the rafters, at a precise row of skis, when I hear a guy's voice. "Lose something?"

"Uh, no." My face floods as I realize he was making a joke. He doesn't seem to notice.

"Once I lost a cat up in the ceiling of our house," he says. "In the heating vents, you know? We could hear it, yowling. We had to open up the vent to get it, and when we did the cat fell right out onto my dad's head."

He has straight brown hair and he's taller than I am, and when he talks he bobs his head a little. Not gorgeous, no way, but not hideous, either.

"Uh-huh," I say.

He's putting his hands in his pockets and is looking over at the workbench. Then he looks back at me.

"I lost a sister, too, but not for near long enough. We left her in the washroom of a gas station. Didn't realize she wasn't in the van until we were twenty minutes up the road." He's laughing.

"Uh-huh." I don't think it's very funny, really.

"But she was fine. We went back and she was sitting on the counter eating ice cream, enjoying all the fuss." He's looking at me. "I have four sisters." He's waiting for something from me.

"Uh-huh?"

"Well, anyway, let me know if you need anything." He's looking over at the workbench, planning his escape.

"Actually, I lost a brother, too." I blurt it out and my voice bounces off the concrete floor, way too loud. "But I haven't got him back yet. My dad took him. No one knows where they are."

"Your dad?" His smile is gone.

"Yeah. He's got this depression thing, and sometimes he doesn't think too clearly."

"Why didn't he take you too?"

His question hits me under the ribs. Maybe Dad meant to and just forgot I'd changed schools. Maybe he tried but couldn't find me. Maybe he didn't want to. I can tell by the guy's face what he's thinking before he even says it.

"My old man is a butthead, too."

He takes my hand and gives it a squeeze. "Feel free to hang here whenever you want. No one's around in the day-time. There's a key over the door."

I watch him as he walks back to the workbench.

After the last time, in case Dad took us again, Mom got a cell phone just for emergencies. If she's out, or at work, she can call-forward the home phone. She drilled our phone number into both of us: zero, then the area code, then the number. Not too fast. Not too slow. She took us to phone booths so we'd know how to work them. She told us how to reach the operator. She even taught us how to ask for help in Spanish and French. Now Mom keeps moaning. "He hasn't called. Why won't he call?"

I know why. But I'd never say it to Mom. Elliott is having a good time. He'll be going to museums and read-ing away rainy afternoons in libraries and eating guy-food and talking, hours and hours, just talking, he and Dad. Because Elliott knows, this is it. He was only five when Mom and Dad split up, not even six when a supervisor began sitting in on our visits. And on some level, he knows that this is it for Dad and him. He's soaking up his father, putting him into every cell of his body, every neuron, downloading Dad into his soul because when he makes that call, Dad will be gone. One way or the other, Dad is out of his life.

And here I am with a bent mother, no brother, in a room full of strangers. I'm not sure I'd be making the phone call, either.

"That's Mike." Ravin's voice cuts in to my thoughts. I've been staring at him and I feel my cheeks flush.

Ravin is watching Mike at the workbench. "I found him last year. He was getting harassed at school because of his clothes. Among other things."

I look at Mike's jeans — cowboy jeans, complete with the fake leather patch. And black Velcro shoes.

"What do you mean, you found him?"

Ravin shrugs. "Found him, rescued him. You know. Like I found you."

I look around at the people in the garage. There's a couple of Sikh kids, a guy out of the slide-rule crowd, a girl with a plaid shirt done up to her chin. No one really matches anyone else.

"So what's this?" I say. "The pound?"

Ravin doesn't crack a smile. "Better hope not. At the pound, we'd be gassed."

"What do you call yourselves?"

She looks at me and her eyes narrow. "What, you mean like Goth-Jock-Nerd?" She laughs derisively and rolls her eyes. "Uh-uh. We're just people. We don't have to conform to anyone else and for sure not to the mainstream groups at James Last."

She leaves me to talk to someone else.

So this is my destiny, or, as Elliott would say, my density. To be rescued by a group of loners, to be alone among them. I wonder when Ravin first pegged me as one of them?

The music is good. I drink Coke, wander around the garage, watch the amazing gyrations of Cor and Julian. People filter in and out in ones and twos. Ravin speaks to everyone. A bookish kid named Nevkeet joins me and talks at great length about the health hazards of processed food. I wonder if he sees the Cheezie crumbs on my shirt. Then he makes his way over to the workbench but I notice he doesn't stay there long.

The music has been notched up through the evening and now thuds through the concrete floor. The voices by the workbench are loud, their words like punches. One boy is swearing, his face so red it looks like he might cry. "They have no right. No way. They can't do this to us."

Mike cuts in. He's not as loud as the others, but when he starts talking, the others get quiet. I can barely hear what he's saying, something about "on their knees."

Ravin comes up beside me, watching them. "That Mike, he's intense." Then she turns and looks at me. "He doesn't have any sisters." There is the smallest of smiles on her face. To the lump of Cor and Julian she calls, "Come on, we've gotta go." Then to me, "The old lady is probably waiting out front."

Cor and Julian emerge dazed from beside the weed whacker (labeled and outlined). Julian looks over to the workbench. The huddle of guys is still clustered around Mike, listening. Julian hesitates.

"Maybe I'll walk home," he says, and his eyes slide back to the workbench.

Cor plants her hands on her hips.

Ravin turns to him, as if she hasn't heard. "C'mon, Julian. It's your turn to ride shotgun."

He nods and, with one last look at the workbench, sheepishly slides his arm around Cor. I follow them out behind Ravin.

No one seems to notice that we're leaving.

CHAPTER SIX

~~~~

Except for the party, it was like the weekend didn't happen, unless watching your mother watching the phone counts as a weekend. Monday at school I saw Cor and Julian in the hall and they waved to me. It could happen that I actually have friends at high school. Not that friends mean much, without Elliott. I can't face returning home after school, to him not being there, so I go to see Chuck at his workroom.

"Is it hard, burying the young ones?"

"Oh, Marlie, don't be going there." Chuck straightens the sheet over a client before wheeling the table into the cold room.

"No, really. I mean, do you feel them around you? Sad little spirits dead before their time?"

Chuck comes back to the table and removes his gloves with a snap. "Your makeup is looking better today." He rummages in the tray beside him and comes up with a nail file. "Want me to do your nails?"

"You have something purple?"

He looks at the back of the tray. "I've got this." He

holds up a bottle of polish — *Amethyst Dawn*. I stretch out my hand. The file scrapes efficiently over my nails. I examine Chuck's bald spot on the top of his head.

"So?"

He looks at me. "So what?"

"So, do you ever feel ghosts? Ghosts of the young?"

He pushes back the cuticles with the end of the file.

"Ow!"

"If you did this once in a while yourself, Marlie, the cuticle wouldn't look like its own life form." He takes sharp clippers and cleans up around my nails. He's working quietly, then he says, "If you were a ghost, would you hang around the undertaker?"

"Yes, to make sure they didn't bury me in anything with frills."

He sets the clippers down and shakes the bottle of polish. He's thinking. I can tell.

"When Dad had the business, a young girl died. She was my age at the time, about sixteen. She looked perfectly normal, but she was slow, something wrong with her brain. Annie. That was her name. You'd see her in the grocery store, and she'd be following her mother around, a little smile on her face. Her mother dressed her really plain — dark-colored dresses and these awful plaid skirts, but she was pretty. Anyone could see that."

"What happened to her?"

Chuck pauses. "She fell. Under a train."

"Ooh."

"Yeah, it was horrible. She and her brother were walking down by the tracks and a train came. Have you ever stood real close to a moving train? It's like it wants to draw you in. Apparently she got scared and started to run. Her brother tried to stop her, but she was out of control. She tripped, fell under the wheels." Chuck drops his head. "It would have been very quick."

"Well, I guess so. Her brother must have felt awful."

Chuck is quiet, brushing the polish onto my nails. "Don't move while that dries." He tightens the cap on the bottle and puts it back in the tray, tidying the other bottles. "Anyway, Dad had her all laid out for the funeral, in some dreadful dark green thing I remember, and I came down here to see her. I knew her brother Mark from school, but he was really a friend of my brother's — a couple of years older than I was. Dad had done a nice job with her. She had just a little pink on her mouth and she wasn't smiling but I could see her smile, that sweet simple smile she always had. She looked peaceful. I was sitting there, just looking at her, and I heard these words. It's not like I heard them with my ears. They were words in my head." He looks at my nails. "That color's not bad. I'm gonna top-coat it so it lasts longer." He digs for a bottle of clear stuff.

"What words? What words?" I demand impatiently.

Chuck is unscrewing the cap. "'I didn't fall.'"

My armpits prickle. "'I didn't fall?'"

Chuck is brushing on the topcoat. "'I didn't fall'. No one thought for a minute that it wasn't an accident. We buried her that afternoon and that was the end of it.

"Her brother, Mark, was an honor student, played on the school football team, a real achiever. After his sister died, he left town, went to school somewhere in Washington State. Then, just a couple of years ago, he was brought up on charges. Against a thirteen-year-old girl."

Chuck shakes his head, disgust written in his eyes.

The workroom feels colder than usual. "So, Mark pushed Annie?"

Chuck shrugs. "Maybe his hands weren't on her, but he pushed her all the same."

I'm holding my fingers outstretched so the polish can set. Chuck swivels my stool so I'm facing him and stares at me hard. "Marlie, don't ever let it get so bad."

I don't know why that makes me mad. Does he think I'm going to jump in front of a train?

"No one is messing with me."

"I know."

"You don't know."

"Okay, I don't know. But you're vulnerable right now, and people can mess with our heads just like they mess with our bodies."

"Who?" I'm really mad now. I hate that he thinks I'm some kind of victim. "Spit it out, Chuck. Who's messing with my head? Dad? My friends? You, like right now?" I'm sorry as soon as I've said it. He looks like I've kicked him.

"Marlie . . ."

I push off my stool without looking at him. All the way to the door I feel him watching me, and I don't look back, because I know what he looks like, his shoulders rounded, all the heart gone from him. I know what he looks like, because it's exactly how I feel right now.

CHAPTER SEVEN

Mom is back at work now. With her bleary eyes and mournful face, she fits right in at the funeral home. At first it was a relief, not having her in the house, clinging to the phone. But then, in the quiet of the house I started hearing footsteps, Elliott's footsteps, and that's scared me so badly that I'd rather do anything than go home. Ravin's house seems as good a place as any. She barely shrugs when I fall in with her after school.

Her house is huge, a white-carpeted maze of foyer and study and breakfast room. Cor and Julian arrive soon after and throw themselves on the white leather couch, their faces planted together. Cor crosses one leg over Julian's. Ravin gets on the phone in the other room, her voice low.

An arrangement of photos on the mantel in the family room catches my eye. They all hold images of a golden-haired girl, a figure skater. In one she's clasping a big silver trophy, smiling. Her front teeth are missing. Another one, taken a few years later, shows her on a podium with two other skaters, a ribboned gold medal around her neck. Her hand is resting on the shoulder of the skater in silver position, a girl with brown curls barely contained in a braid. They're smiling at each other, radiant.

"Quite the geek, wasn't I?" Ravin is standing behind me, her hands on her hips, bony elbows like clothespins. I didn't hear her come up.

"This is you?" My mouth is gaping, but I can't help it. The thought of Ravin in one of those flippy little figure-skater costumes makes me want to laugh. Not that I'd laugh at Ravin.

"I was good, really. Very good." She takes a framed certificate from the mantel and hands it to me. It reads, "Divisional Champion, Ravin Hughes." It's dated three years ago.

"Wow." I hand it back to her. I look for more photos, more certificates, but there are none. "Do you have others?"

"No. I quit not long after I got this." She jams the certificate in behind a set of candlesticks on the mantel. "This is my mother's shrine to all those early mornings at the rink. She hasn't quite forgiven me." Ravin picks up the photo of the girls on the podium and stabs with her finger the head of the brown-haired girl. "That's Lindsay Hammon. You've heard of her."

I repeat the name. "I don't think so."

"You will then. She'll skate in the Olympics."

"The Olympics! You were even better than her?"

She narrows her eyes. "I was. Not anymore, obviously." She plunks the photo back down.

"So why did you quit?"

Ravin's shoulders tighten.

"You don't have to tell me. Not if you don't want to."

She looks at me and shakes her head. "It was just

stupid, really. Lindsay and I were unbeatable. We had the best coaches from the best clubs. But then a rabid skating mom with too much time and money on her hands started lobbying for more coaching for her kid. Other skaters were cut back, and that still wasn't enough. People were fighting with one another, and the mothers," she rolls her eyes, "they were the worst. So to protest, Lindsay and I agreed to do something outrageous, something that would embarrass the club. Lindsay dyed her hair bright red; I went black. And we got pierced." She points to her eyebrow. "It shouldn't have mattered what we looked like. But it always does."

"You were brave."

Ravin laughs a little. "Lindsay, with her red hair, she looked like Anne of Green Gables." Then her smile fades. "She showed up at competition without the ring; with her hair back to her normal color. She said her mother made her do it. Maybe she had. Mine wasn't too pleased with me, that's for sure. Anyway, I got what I deserved."

"They gave you lower marks? Just because of how you looked?"

"No. They gave me lower marks because I fell on a jump I'd been landing since I was nine. Maybe I was mad, maybe I was just losing my edge. But I didn't even make it to the podium. Lindsay took home the gold medal and hasn't looked back since."

"Are you still friends?"

"Maybe we were never really friends. Maybe it was just about skating."

The doorbell rings and for a minute Ravin stands there, looking at the photo, like she hasn't heard it. Then she says, "Skating became too much like work. I packed it in. Anyway," she sighs, looking at me, "it was the principle of the thing." With a small shake of her head, she goes to answer the door.

I stand a moment more, looking at the pictures of Ravin with her blonde hair. Elliott, when he was about four, used to get his words mixed up. Once he wandered through the house with his hands over his eyes, bumping into furniture, saying, "I'm blond, I'm blond!" Mom and I laughed so hard. With one last glance at the photographs, I follow Ravin out to the foyer.

In the living room, Cor and Julian shift on the couch, their faces still glued. I think about those lamprey eels, with the mouths that are their whole head. Maybe Cor and Julian are actually stuck together. Air-locked or something. Big, burly firefighters will have to come and pry them apart. STAND BACK, FOLKS. WE'RE GOING TO HAVE TO USE THE JAWS OF LIFE.

"What are you staring at?"

My face floods. Mike and some other guys are coming in the front door. He pokes me in the side.

"I've got to log on." He takes the stairs up two at a time. He seems to know his way around pretty well.

The other guys are starting to disperse. Against the stark whiteness of Ravin's house they look like exclamation marks. One of them heads for the kitchen. I hear the fridge opening. Several flop down on the couch in the living room. Cor and Julian are oblivious. A guy with a hank of hair over his eyes flips the pages of a fancy coffee-table book, *New England's Covered Bridges*. He picks at a zit on his nose while he's reading.

From upstairs Mike calls, "Hey, Ravin, how's your cat?"

"You've got a cat?" I say. "I love cats."

The guys are laughing. "Yeah. Mike likes cats, too," one of them says. It's the one with the book. "He likes them microwa—"

"Shut up." Ravin's voice is low, measured. The laughter stops. He flips her a rude gesture.

"Mike didn't turn it on, Marlie." She says it like I ought to know that.

"Or the time he got your old lady's gun and begged you to let him off the cat."

Abruptly, Cor and Julian disengage. Cor says, "I didn't know your mom had a gun."

Ravin shrugs. "My dad works a lot of night shifts. It was either a dog or a gun." She gazes pointedly at the white upholstery, the careful arrangement of art and ornaments, the expanse of linen on the table in the dining room. "Strangely, she chose a gun."

"Where does she keep it?" Cor asks.

Ravin is getting bored. "By her bed. Where else?"

"Can I see it?"

"You're weird." But she makes for the stairs. Cor gets off the couch to follow her and I follow Cor.

I go with them into Ravin's parents' room. I can smell her parents in that plush white space and recognize her mother in the old pictures on the wall. Ravin opens her mother's bedside drawer. Inside, there's a folded embroidered hanky. Ravin flips it aside to reveal a handgun.

Cor gasps and Ravin laughs. "Want to hold it?" She lifts it from the drawer and offers it to Cor.

"No." Cor snatches her hands behind her back.

My mouth has gone totally dry.

Ravin takes my hand and folds it around the gun.

"Don't go shooting yourself with it." Then she spins on her heel and leaves.

I don't know how long I hold it. I'm just as afraid to put it down. It amazes me, its weight, the coldness of the steel, the absolute absence of color or light in the shape of it.

Cor finally breaks its spell. "You're getting sweat all over the gun."

We giggle, a crazy, scared giggle and, together, set the gun back into the drawer.

I wipe my hands on my pants and follow Cor back downstairs. She plunks down on the couch beside Julian.

"I need a drink of water," I say and retreat to the kitchen. My knees feel like Jell-O. The guy in the fridge is eating olives out of the jar, sucking out the red pimento part then chewing the olive with an open mouth. His hands are filthy. I glance into the adjoining family room. Mike has come back down, talking on a portable phone. His back is to me, and he's walking while he's talking.

"If one is all you can get, that'll have to do. It just takes one, isn't that what they say?" He laughs. "I'll tell you where." He clicks the phone off.

The guy in the fridge is drinking orange juice, tipping the jug so it pours into his mouth. A dribble runs off his chin and disappears down his neck. My water glass is halfway to my mouth. I feel Mike's stare before I see it; the hairs on my arms stand up. He's looking at me, and his eyes are as black as his jacket. With his thumb and forefinger he makes a gun and aims it at my head.

"Bang, bang. You're dead."

CHAPTER EIGHT

—⁓—

Mike and Ravin come to the library Monday with burgers and Cokes for us all. I'd been trying to complete an overdue Social Studies assignment. I'd had all weekend to do it, but I can't seem to concentrate on homework. Mom worked both afternoons, and I hate the emptiness of Elliott's room and how the house alternates between dead quiet and echoing with ghostly whispers. Last night I gave up and went for a walk. I walked to the elementary school, the same way I'd walked for eight years, the same way Elliott walked, the very last time he did it. The familiar compact houses with their tidy front lawns and warmly lit windows only made me feel lonelier. I'm happy for some company.

Mike tells us this funny story about his driver's ed. teacher, about how his hands shake and he smells like he's dead. I tell them about Chuck. Mike can't believe I know an undertaker.

"Does he have a hump, like Igor?"

"No. He wears khaki pants and button-up shirts."

"So, do you think he has a thing for dead bodies?"

"That's disgusting."

"Are he and your mom, you know?" He raises his eyebrows suggestively.

"That's more disgusting." Actually, that's one of my favorite fantasies, that Chuck and Mom will fall in love. I know Chuck would never make a play for Mom, not ever. Because of Dad. Too bad.

"You going to eat that?" Mike reaches over and bites a huge hunk out of my burger. It makes a lump in his cheek and moves from one side of his mouth to the other. Then, still with the lump of burger in his mouth, he takes a big slurp of my Coke. There are floaties in my Coke, I know without even looking.

"I WAS going to eat it."

"Want it back?" He opens his mouth to reveal the gray mass. This is so much like Elliott. Suddenly I get a stab of pain. I miss him, a lot.

This morning Mr. Bates, the school counselor, called me into his office. Mr. Bates always wears a turtleneck under a sweater, and he perches on things. The side of a desk, the ledge under the white board, a bookshelf. He has long legs that bend like a grasshopper's. He's a tireless warrior for students' rights. If a student wants something that the administration is not going to like, he goes first to Mr. Bates. I've heard that Mrs. Birk detests him.

I knew he wanted to check my mental health, but he was nice about it.

"This is a big school, Marlie. It can take awhile for ninth-grade students to break in. Some of our students find they need some help. I hope you'll always feel that this door is open to you."

"Thanks. But I'm fine."

He smiles at me. "Ms. Grimshaw tells me you're a great help to her."

"Oh."

"That you remind her of herself in high school." Oh that's comforting.

"We're on your side, Marlie. Let us help you, if you need it."

Just wave your wand, Mr. Bates, and magic my brother home.

As the bell rings, Ravin asks me if I've had any more trouble with Loren.

"Loren who?" Mike says.

I tell him. "Loren Miller. She's on the volleyball team."

"Not anymore," Ravin says. "She got tossed off for spiking a ball in the face of a line ref. Apparently she didn't like how the ref had called a ball."

"Typical jock behavior." Mike's face shows disgust.

"Not really," Ravin retorts. "It's typical idiot behavior. She was an idiot before she was an athlete."

Mike snorts. "All jocks are losers."

Ravin rolls her eyes at him, but doesn't argue any further.

I say, "How do you know about Loren getting thrown from the team?"

She half-laughs. "I spend way too much time at the office. I heard Coach Wallen talking to Fiona."

"You're not thinking about rescuing Loren too, are you?"

She slaps me gently in the side of the head. "I don't think so, not Loren. She's too fiery. But if you'd like me to . . ." She smiles.

"No. Please don't."

Mike and Ravin walk me up to science. Mike comes right in, like he owns the place. The class is just going to start, and there are people milling around.

"Meet after school, down by the wood shop," he says in a low voice. "Everyone will be there."

A big kid doing Ninth Grade, The Sequel, gets up from his station and starts moving toward Mike. He has pure white hair and lumbers rather than walks. His arms curve like barrel staves at his sides and his T-shirt strains across his chest. A small crest on the sleeve reads, "James Last Secondary School Football Team." He's eyeing Mike with barely concealed disgust.

"Get 'im, Lex. Sic 'im," the guys are hooting and cheering.

Mr. Inkster, the height-challenged chemistry teacher, is just coming in the door, his arms full of papers and a tray of test tubes. Mike slips out beside him.

"Take your seats!" Mr. Inkster's voice squeaks above the rabble. "Immediately!" Lex turns ponderously and makes his way back to his spot.

A voice comes clearly through the scraping of chairs and thumping of textbooks, a girl's voice this time. "Who would want anything to do with that creep?"

"They'd make the perfect couple." Loud laughter.

"Students! You will come to order!" Mr. Inkster is erasing the board, his little arm pumping like a piston over long strings of numbers and letters. I turn to the voices. An army of blue tracksuits are looking at me over their noses.

I should do what I always do and turn away. Ignore them. That's what the teachers say. If you react, you only encourage them. And if you fight, then you're as bad as they are. I turn in my seat so I can face them square on. I know she's there, Keely Willson. And I know she's smirking, just like the rest of them. But I let my eyes mark each face, moving slowly from one to another, tracking each perky pony to the next, until I reach Keely. And when I reach Keely, I pause an extra long time. Her cheeks color a little, but she rolls her eyes and leans back in her chair with her arms crossed.

"Page ninety-eight, students." Mr. Inkster is squeaking into the board. "That's nine-eight." The class is still rumbling. "Immediately!" Textbooks slam open and pages are turned.

My eyes fix on Keely's. I know everything about her. I know what she eats for breakfast. That she uses hot water on her toothbrush. That she got her ears pinned back when she was six. That her Uncle Rhys has got some funny ideas of how little girls should hug. She doesn't look anything like me, but when I look in Keely's face, it's like looking in a mirror. I know her that well. I raise my thumb and forefinger and aim them at her head.

"Bang, bang. You're dead."

CHAPTER NINE

The wood shop corridor is empty when I get there. I stand around, pretending to read the bulletin board with such interesting notices as "SAFETY FIRST. ALWAYS WEAR YOUR HEARING PROTECTION." And a notice about extra shop time on Friday to learn something called "biscuit joinery." I'm beginning to think I'm in the wrong hall when Ravin sprints up, her white face dotted with pink from running.

"It's Nevkeet." She pants out the words, her eyes bright with excitement. "They got Nevkeet."

I follow her out, running hard. At Mike's party, Nevkeet told me he wants to be an astronaut. He's obviously brilliant — he's in tenth grade, but studies physics and math two grades higher. In his spare time he plays violin. I don't know what Nevkeet's greater crime is — his weird name or that somehow, in some small, barely perceptible way, he revealed to others what everyone feels but must never show. That he is afraid. I can see Mike and the others behind the automotive shop doors. Mike is cursing, pacing back and forth on the pavement, his fists clenched. I can't keep up with Ravin. She runs like a racer. Sweat is pouring off me and I have to walk. Cor and Julian are standing to one side, watching Mike. I'm the last to get there.

Nevkeet is sitting on a curb, his head in his hands. Ravin is crouched down next to him.

"How did they get you, Nevkeet? Why were you alone?"

Nevkeet glances at Mike, then back to Ravin. His left eye is blue and puffy. There's dried blood under his nose. His violin is a crumpled mess, held together by its strings. Nevkeet is cradling it in his lap. He shrugs.

"You've got to get something on that eye. Come on, I'll walk you in to see Coach Schroeder. He'll have some ice." Ravin starts to help Nevkeet up.

"No." Mike swats Ravin's hand off of Nevkeet. "No. He's not going back into that school. Not looking like that." Mike shoves Nevkeet back down to the curb. Everyone is silent.

"There are going to be a few changes in this school." Mike's voice is controlled now — and cold. Julian moves in next to him. "This act will not go unpunished." Mike is reciting injustices delivered to individuals of the group. "It's us against them, my friends. One army. One force for change. For justice."

I look over at Ravin. Her white-blue eyes are glued to Mike. Round red spots color her pale cheeks. She's chewing on a thumbnail. I have a sudden picture of her in her skating costume, waiting for her marks to come up.

Mike is searching our faces in turn, as if to detect any defiance, any weakness. "One by one and by the hundred." He faces me. I force myself not to look down, not to look away. Everyone else seems to be watching me, too. Mike's eyes feel like knuckles. I suck in a breath, taking the energy of his eyes, willing mine open, praying for his to turn. He holds me with his stare, beats me with it, until I can hardly breathe. "By the hundred and by the thousand." He smiles. "We will make them pay."

CHAPTER TEN

~~~

Shoulders and hips jostle in the locker room, with one flush-cheeked class finishing up, and the other just coming in. I unlock my tote box and reach for my gym strip. I grab my stuff and head for a toilet cubicle to change. I hate gym days. Gym class ruins a perfectly good Friday.

Not enough room in here to change your mind. That's what Chuck would say. The toilet gapes like an open mouth, ready to swallow anything that I drop. The latch on the door pokes me in the rump when I bend over. I'm already in a sweat and gym class hasn't even started.

I'm sitting on the toilet, doing up my running shoes, when I hear Loren's voice. She's in the class before mine, and normally I can get changed and out of the locker room before she gets in. Not today. She's in front of the sinks, just outside my door.

"We should have won today." Her voice is hard, angry. I hear water running, and in the crack of the door I see more people clustered around the sinks. Great, I'm trapped.

"Yeah," another voice says, "why did we get stuck with that loser?"

"Coach Wallen's idea of fair play." Oh, great. Just wonderful. It's Keely. "Make us play with a total waste of skin. She couldn't even return the ball, much less set it up for you."

I've got to get out of here or I'll be late. Being late for gym means extra laps or, heaven help me, push-ups. I wait for a diversion.

"They hit it right to her. We didn't have a hope."

"Ssh, here she comes."

"I don't care if she hears me." Loren's voice is dangerous. "Jeez, nice effort out there. Do you think you could have given them any more points?"

Through the door crack I can't see who they're railing at, but they're turned away from me. This is my chance. I gather my clothes into a heap, grab my shoes in one hand, my gym binder in the other. With the one finger that is free, I unbolt the door.

Loren and the others have circled the girl. I don't know her. In her gym strip she looks like everyone else, but the haunted look in her eyes marks her as prey. Loren is jabbing at her.

"I don't like to lose, loser. And you made me lose."

The girl knocks Loren's hand away.

"Whooo. Tough female." Loren's face is bright red.

The girl is trying to shoulder her way through the horde.

"Don't make that mistake again." Loren's foot strikes out, hitting the girl in the shin. She cries out in pain. Loren is drawing her foot back, ready to kick her again.

"Okay, okay. I hear you." The girl is angry. She looks like she might cry. The others move back just enough to let her out.

"Loser," Loren says, to her back. "Only exercise she gets is bending down to kiss my butt."

A shoe drops from my hand. Loren turns to the sound, then they all do. I bend down to get the shoe and my jeans slip onto the floor. When I try to get the jeans, my other shoe falls. I'm grabbing everything, holding it in a heap against my chest. I'm aware of their energy, now turned to me. I draw slowly up. Their ugliness isn't done.

Keely is moving toward me, a sneer on her face. "You in the habit of hanging around, listening to other people's conversations?"

Loren steps in close, her face just inches from mine. "You weren't spying, were you?" Her arm comes up fast and knocks everything in my arms onto the floor. "Oh, here, let me help you with that." With a deft kick, she sends my sweatshirt flying, right into a toilet. The others shriek with laughter.

I gather my stuff again, leaving the sweatshirt. I don't have time, anyway. Keely is bent double laughing. I bolt out of the sink area, into the main locker room toward the door. I've got to take everything with me or I'll be late. As I shove open the door, I look back. The girl is sitting on the bench, changing. She looks up at me. There's nothing in her eyes that says anything happened. There's nothing to say she saw what happened to me. She's invisible. Sitting on the bench, one leg in her pants, she's not even there. There are others in the locker room, but they haven't looked up. Maybe I'm not here, either.

❖ ❖ ❖

Just before afternoon classes, a fire alarm clamors in the stairwell. People's voices get quiet for a moment as they figure out what it is, then become loud and excited.

Cor and Julian slip in beside me. "It's not a fire drill," Cor says. "SOMEONE set off a smoke bomb in the office."

"A bomb?" A squeaky-voiced guy next to Cor almost shouts it. The tone in the crowd changes to strident questioning.

"There's a bomb? Someone planted a bomb."

"Where did it go off? Was anyone hurt?"

Cor looks at me and rolls her eyes. "We'll be out for the afternoon. We can sit in the gym down the hill." She motions with her head to Elliott's school. "Or we can cut to my house, just the other side of the field. You can practically see it from here."

Teachers are directing everyone away from the school. Sirens are screaming and every fire truck and police car in the district is piling up in front of the school.

"Your house, definitely." I fall into step with her and Julian.

Julian hesitates. "Actually, I'm supposed to meet up with Mike."

Cor stops. "So let's go."

He shakes his head. "Uh, no. Just me."

Cor glances at me and her face reddens. She turns back to Julian, her mouth an angry knot. "Fine." Then without another word to Julian, she grabs me and stalks off.

I don't know how many brothers and sisters Cor has, but her house looks like a Fisher-Price commercial gone bad. The kitchen table is littered with sippy cups and crumbs, and the floor is a minefield of plastic bits and pieces.

"What are you doing home?" Her mother is balancing a half-clothed toddler on her hip, an empty baby bottle in her hand, and a wild-haired little girl is hanging off her leg. Somewhere, a TV is blaring daytime talk. The toddler is drooling thin streams onto a dirty T-shirt.

"Bomb scare. They sent us home."

Cor's mother looks up at the ceiling and shakes her head. "Well, since you're home, you could . . ."

Cor pushes me toward the basement steps. "I brought a friend. We've got to study."

Cor's mother looks at me then, as if she hasn't noticed that I've been standing there the whole time. Cor yanks the basement door closed behind us.

The basement smells. It's dark, and I feel my way behind Cor through a maze of cardboard boxes, old clothes, and ancient appliances. Cor's "room" is a curtained cubicle in the corner. She pulls a chain and light floods over us.

The bed is made with a taut pink bedspread. A set of shelves nailed on the wall studs holds books, neatly sorted. An old doll with bad hair leans against the books. The floor is covered with a braided rug, and under a small window there is a wooden desk and chair.

Cor steps up on the chair, then onto the desk. She opens the window and a fresh breeze circulates. She leans on the edge of the window.

"This is the fire escape. It's big enough to climb out."

"Or in."

Cor laughs and jumps down. "Well, I wouldn't know about that."

"So how do you know Mike planted the smoke bomb?"

"Did I say Mike planted it?" Cor puts a look of fake innocence on her face.

"No, you didn't."

I pick up a magazine from beside the bed. The cover shows a guy shot through the heart. "True Crimes? Since when did you become a True Crimes fan?"

Cor takes the magazine from me and tosses it on a shelf. "What are you, Ms. Grimshaw's secret agent?" She purses her lips and makes her eyes wild. "STUDENTS, TIME IS PRECIOUS. DO NOT WASTE IT READING MEANINGLESS TRASH. And why are you still wearing your gym shirt?"

I tell her about Loren. She shakes her head.

"So what's Mike's plan?" I say. "There's not a real bomb, is there?"

Cor shoots me a look. "He's just making a statement. But who cares? We get a free afternoon out of the deal."

I sit on the very edge of her bed. "Do you think there'd ever be a real bomb? I've heard there are sites on the Net with instructions on how to make them."

"Why would Mike do something like that?" She laughs, but it doesn't sound real.

"I don't know. There's that thing with Nevkeet." I shiver in my T-shirt.

"Mike likes to talk big." She flops onto the chair by the desk.

The sound of the TV drones through the floorboards, and one of the kids is crying. I can hear harried footsteps back and forth overhead. Cor is sitting at the desk, her arms at her side, staring blankly up at the window.

CHAPTER ELEVEN

—⌇⌇—

When I get home, it's already dark. Mom is sitting in her chair, her head tilted back, a pink washcloth folded over her eyes. She doesn't say anything when I come in. Maybe she's asleep. There's nothing in the sink tonight, no frozen chunk of beast, no freezer tray of supermarket lasagna. No clues as to what she was thinking about for supper. I get out bread and peanut butter. The bread is freckled with fuzzy green mold. I heave it into the trash. I eat a blob of peanut butter off the end of the knife. Chuck comes through the front door, and with him, the scent of KFC. Mom lifts up the washcloth.

"Fair damsels, 'tis I, Sir Charles, back from the wars, with booty, too." He drops a huge barrel of fried chicken on the kitchen table. From under his arm he pulls a bottle of Welch's Grape Juice. "Marlie, grab some glasses." From the pockets of his enormous overcoat he pulls two red-and-white containers and sets them on the table with a flourish. "Gravy. Nectar of the gods."

Mom is smiling at Chuck. Her eyes are red and puffy. He fills the glasses with the grape juice and touches his to

Mom's. "Cheers." He drains his glass, then sits down. "Ooh, plates. That's a nice touch."

I fold a paper towel by each spot. Chuck has peeled open the barrel and holds it out for Mom and me. Mom takes a piece with her fingertips. I take two and set them on my plate. Chuck dunks his into the gravy then tears into it. Mom uses her knife and fork to peel back all the skin from her piece before cutting it into little pieces. Chuck is on his third piece.

"Oh, I shoulda got some salad." He tosses me a packet of ketchup. "Here, Marlie, eat your vegetables."

I dunk my drumstick into the gravy. Not bad. Chuck tilts the barrel for me to reach another piece. A pile of bones covers his plate. He's dipping rolls into the gravy now, wiping the sides of the container to get every drop. Mom is dabbing at her mouth with the paper towel. Chuck pours more grape juice into the glasses and leans back in his chair. There are two pieces of chicken left in the barrel. I get up to put it in the fridge.

"I'll clean this up later," Mom says. "Why don't you start on your homework?" Her hands are fluttering on the neckline of her sweater.

"I'll come see you before I leave." Chuck tilts his juice glass to me, like a toast.

"Thanks, Chuck. For the dinner. You know."

He waves me off. "Yeah, yeah. That's Sir Charles, to you."

Homework. I have a bag full of it for the weekend. It's the last thing I feel like doing. On the way to my room I pause at Elliott's open door. It's exactly the way he left it. His pencils stand neatly in a cup on his desk. His bookshelf is sorted: dinosaurs and birds on one shelf; blood and guts on another. I can almost smell him in this room, his sweet baby smell. I go in and sit on the little chair by his bed and pick up the book he was reading. The cover shows a turreted castle, with brave-looking knights in the foreground and a band of black-caped marauders storming toward them.

Earlier this week, at the library, Cor came in just before the bell and signed out a book of the same series. Hers showed a princess in a white helmet swinging a broad sword at an evil-looking knight. There was a burning castle in the background. Cor looked a little embarrassed to be signing it out. "I read this book ages ago. I just want to read it again."

Elliott is a good reader, but still, it's probably a little young for Cor. "Yeah," I said. "I read the whole series."

She looked relieved.

"This one was my favorite." I imitated the voice of the wicked knight, "I'll 'ave your 'eart with my evenin' tea, and the rest of you too, if it pleases me."

Cor laughed. "I liked the peasant scouts, the way they're noble without trying to be."

"But the women that they call witches," I said. "What's with them? They're the smartest creatures in the kingdom but they're always pawns for the bad guys."

Cor shrugged. "No power."

"They've got psychic power. They can see the future. And they have healing power."

Cor shook her head. "No fire power. They do what they have to, just to survive."

I look up from Elliott's book to see Chuck leaning in the doorway. I close the book and set it back down on the chair.

"Chuck, I'm sorry about blowing up at you."

"Forget it."

"I miss him, you know?"

Chuck comes and hugs me. He smells of fried chicken. I put my arms around his soft middle and hug him back. It feels strange. I can't remember the last time I hugged my dad. Suddenly I'm crying. Dad won't be back. Not this time. Not for me and Elliott. Chuck is crying as well.

"I know, Marlie. I miss them, too."

CHAPTER TWELVE

—◆—

"What stinks in here?" Julian is sniffing at the air, his nose wrinkled. For a minute I think he's taking a shot at me.

"It's books, Julian." Cor looks at me and rolls her eyes. "This is a library. This is what books smell like."

"I don't like it. It smells weird." He sniffs some more. "Maybe that's why no one ever comes here. They're afraid they're gonna catch something."

No one does come here. Not at lunch, anyway. Or, rather, no one *used to* come here. Mike, Ravin, and five or six others have been hanging out in the library at lunch all this week. If it was Nevkeet, I wouldn't mind so much. He'd probably take out a book and read. But these guys are just loud. It makes me uncomfortable. I liked it better when I was alone.

"Man, is she equipped!" Mike is snooping in Ms. Grimshaw's office, sitting down at her computer.

"You shouldn't be back there."

Mike doesn't look up. "Relax. It's all passworded."

"Yeah, but what if she comes back?"

"Then you'll tell me."

"Yeah, but . . ."

"Yeah, but nothing. You're acting like a baby." He's pulled something up on the screen and his fingers are clattering on the keyboard. He lets out a soft whistle.

"Names, addresses, names of siblings. Everything's here."

I go back behind Ms. Grimshaw's desk to see what he's got on the screen. It's something official looking. A school program.

"I thought you said it was all passworded?"

"It is. Or was. Mrs. Orthney keeps them written under her desk pad. In case she forgets." He bips around on the screen, the cursor moving so fast it makes my head hurt.

"You better get out of there."

"I will. I've just got to download some data."

"Mike, what if they know someone's been in there?" I'm starting to panic now.

"Then they'll think it was Grimshaw." Mike looks up from the keys. He smiles. "Or you."

The others are huddled around a table, laughing over something in *Guinness World Records*. Cor and Julian are in the 600s, linked at the lips. I really want them out of here.

"Come on, Mike. You've got to leave." He doesn't answer.

Then, a sharp *sssst* from Ravin brings my eyes up to the door, to Ms. Grimshaw bustling into the library. Mike dives under the desk.

Ms. Grimshaw's back is to me. She's eyeing the table of boys with the book.

"Exit out!" Mike is glaring at me from under the desk. I look at the computer screen. The school program is gone. Another program is on the screen. It looks like he's dialed into his computer at home.

Ms. Grimshaw is addressing the table. "Are you finding everything all right?" She launches into her favorite topic: the Dewey Decimal System. "Books are all sorted by type, if they are non-fiction, that is. What is it that you are interested in?" She turns the book so that she can read it. "Oh, my. Those are huge. Students, these just aren't normal." Several of the boys snigger into their arms. "But if you REALLY wanted to study anatomy, then you'd find that subject in the shelves marked . . ."

"Exit!" Mike's eyes are frantic under the desk.

I look back at the screen. My hand is on the mouse. Ms. Grimshaw is tutoring on the decimals. "No, no, .001 is BEFORE .01." On the screen is a list, neatly formatted, alphabetical, surname first. It's student names and a dossier of information about their families, unlisted phone numbers, addresses of their parents' work, even their immunization records.

"Just exit, Marlie." Mike has his teeth clenched.

Adams, Brett. He and his buddies like to corner new kids in the washroom and flush their heads in the urinal.

Davidson, Seth. Mike said he saw him follow Nevkeet out that day he got hurt.

Geroux, James. Apparently he posted a "Losers Club" web site and nominated Mike as its president.

Lemley, Lex. That's the big guy from science class.

"Now, if you can't take this seriously you can go outside." Ms. Grimshaw is approaching the end of her lesson.

Manderley, there are three of them, all brothers. I don't know anything about them.

Miller, Loren. I know who that is.

Pryor, Amanda. I heard she went out with Mike. Once.

Russel, Nyles. The president of the student council.

Tremonte, William. Plays every sport known to man. He's huge.

And then my eyes stop. All of these names, all of these people, have apparently committed some crime against Mike. All are on Mike's home computer.

All selected. For what?

Willson, Keely. My ex-best friend.

Mike is worming out from under the desk. I can hear Cor asking Ms. Grimshaw a question, buying us time. "Is Dewey the name of a person, Ms. Grimshaw?"

"Well, yes. As a matter of fact . . ."

Mike's hand is searching the top of the desk for the mouse. He's swearing at me under his breath.

Willson, Keely. Her name on that list is like a rusty nail on my tongue. It doesn't belong there. Not on any list of Mike's. Who knows what he has in mind?

Mike is on his knees, trying to reach the keyboard. "It's just a mailing list," he hisses.

I click on the icon to delete the file.

"You seem genuinely interested in the library. There's another student I'd like you to meet. Marlie?" Ms. Grimshaw is turning toward the desk. Toward her office.

The computer is asking me if I really want to delete the document.

Mike's hand is struggling for the mouse.

I have one eye on Ms. Grimshaw and I'm trying to move

the mouse to OK. "Marlie," Mike says, "you know what some of them did last year?"

Cor is gesturing wildly to us behind Ms. Grimshaw's back. The guys are pouring out of the library.

"Some of those people on the list — you know what they did?"

I look at Mike. His eyes are fierce, shining. My hand on the mouse pauses.

"They broke bones, Marlie."

I feel Mike's hand take the mouse.

"Ask Cor. She knows."

He's not looking at me. His eyes are on the monitor, exiting the program. He's cool, almost like he's enjoying this. He's in control again.

Ms. Grimshaw is giving me a "what are you doing in my office?" look. She must not be able to see Mike behind the stack of books on her desk.

The screen goes blank. Then he crouches again behind the desk.

It's like I hardly have air to breathe. I have to try twice before I find my voice and even then it quavers.

"I'll be right out, Ms. Grimshaw. I'm just getting some tape."

As I'm leaving, I hear Mike. It sounds like he's laughing.

CHAPTER THIRTEEN

mm

I wonder if this is what it feels like, just before you lose your mind. I have absolutely no memory of afternoon classes. It was just the two things rolling around in my head: that list, and the sound of Mike laughing. I don't know which scares me worse. At home, I stand in the entry so long even Mom comes to.

"Open com-link, Marlena." She's watching me from the couch, a puzzled look on her face.

It's an Elliottism. I reward her with a smile, and shake my head to clear it.

"Just a rough day. Science. You know."

She nods, then yawns. "Me too. I'm so tired I can hardly stay awake." She lets her head drop to the pillow and pulls her legs up onto the couch. Her voice becomes slack, "Do want to talk about it?"

"No Mom, that's okay. I'm going to go out for awhile."

I'm not sure she hears me. Her eyes are already closed.

Maybe I've already lost my mind. Elliott would think so, if he knew I was going to see Nana.

Nana isn't your cookies-and-milk kind of grandmother.

She's had two face-lifts and she doesn't even like to be called "grandmother." She lives downtown in a glass-and-chrome high-rise with a tiny white dog called "Prancey." Prancey humps your foot and snaps if you try to pat him. We don't see much of Nana.

But she paid for my braces and she'll pay for college, if I ever get there. Maybe it's a long shot, but I figure if I go see her, maybe she'll let something slip, something about Dad. Nana loves Dad like a she-bear.

The mirrored walls of the elevator reflect my backside in an unflattering three-way display. With my sleeve I give my mouth a swipe.

The doors slide open on the thirty-seventh floor to a vast foyer, the carpet so thick there's an unnerving sense of sinking into it. Three doors open off the foyer, discreetly lit and numbered in gold. Behind my grandmother's door Prancey is having a fit. I stand there, wondering if I should knock. She knows I'm here — I called her from the lobby and she buzzed me up. Tentatively, softly, I knock two times.

Prancey sounds like he's going to have heart failure. Finally, after what seems like a very long time, I hear my grandmother's voice.

"Hush now, baby. Such a good baby." The yapping subsides to an annoying hiccup. The door opens on its chain, then abruptly closes.

For a minute, I think she's changed her mind, that she's not going to see me. But then the door swings open.

Nana is wearing a soft green sweater and slacks the exact same color. Her yellow-blonde hair is piled on her head and her lipstick is precisely lined in a pale shade of peach.

She's stunning, my grandmother.

In her arms she holds the dog, red-eyed and weepy looking, a pouf of white curls. He's growling at me, his sharp little teeth bared in a yellow grimace.

"Well, now, Marlena, won't you come in?" She's smiling just enough to be kind. "Yes, just put your footwear on that bit of paper." She's set out a clean square of brown paper, neatly trimmed on the sides. I hope like anything these socks don't have holes.

I follow her into a designer room of antique rugs and uncomfortable furniture. She motions me to a straight-backed chair by the gas fireplace. She takes a floral wing chair, turning in it slightly to face me.

"How is your dear mother? Such a strain this must be for her." She shakes her head slowly. "And you, are you coping?" She's studying my face, searching for signs of her son in it. Everyone says I look like my father. Nana's never been able to see it.

"I'm fine, Nana. And Mom is okay. How are you? And Prancey?"

"My Prancey darling had to have a mean old operation." She's holding the dog up to her face, and even he looks disgusted. "His poor little tummy was all shaved. I was a wreck." She sets the dog down and it settles into a surly pile beside her. "But he's much better, thank you."

Silence drops between us like a force field. Finally she says, "You must want some tea. I'll make us some."

"No, Nana, really, I just came to . . ." She's already got up and gone to the kitchen. The dog shifts in the chair and eyes me.

When I was younger, before I knew what he was doing,

I didn't mind Prancey humping my foot. I tuck my feet against the chair.

"Do you take sugar and milk?" her voice calls from the kitchen.

"Just however you're having it is fine, Nana." She makes this nasty herb stuff that tastes like compost. The dog jumps down and sniffs my feet.

"Hey, Prancey, old boy." I say it quietly, so my grandmother won't hear. "Leave me alone, okay?" He's nosing my right foot, positioning himself.

"No, Prancey. Think of your stitches." I try to move my foot, but he's quick and snaps at my toes with a growl.

Nana comes in with a tray and sets it down on a low round table, black with varnish. The dog is doing my foot, and I'm red as a tomato, and Nana pours the tea. "One lump or two?"

"Two." I kick my foot a bit, thinking I might disengage the dog. He goes faster.

She hands me a teacup, the handle too small to put a finger through, then a saucer, a napkin, and a plate. There's nothing on the tray to put on the plate, but I take it anyway.

She sits back in her chair, a perfect balance of hairdo and teacup. "You said you needed to see me."

I set down my cup on the edge of the tray. It jiggles with the motion of the dog. "I have something to leave with you. For Elliott. In case Dad calls here."

"Now, Marlena, I told you I hadn't heard from your father."

"I know. But just in case." I reach down to my bag and pull out a package. "It's Elliott's book, the one he was reading. Before he . . . left." I've wrapped it in brown paper.

Her eyes soften at the sight of the package. "You should just take it home with you."

I put it on the table and get up to leave. The dog yips like I've stepped on him.

"Oh, Prancey. Come to Mommy." The dog jumps up beside her and licks himself.

"No. I'm going to leave it here. Because maybe if I leave it here, then he'll call here. It'll be like a talisman or something."

She squirms in the chair. "Oh, this is so hard for everybody."

It's there in her voice and it's there in her eyes that won't meet mine. She's heard from Dad — or expects to.

"Nana, this is hardest for you." I hope my voice sounds convincing. "Mom and I still have each other, and Elliott and Dad have each other." I put my hand on her shoulder as if to console her. "But you, you're the one left all alone."

She nods, wiping at tears.

"He's your only child. He's all you have. You and Prancey."

She's sobbing silently.

"For you, I wish he would come back."

She clasps my hand on her shoulder and gives it a pat.

"You're a good girl," she says, releasing my hand. "It can't hurt anything to leave your parcel." Her eyes drop to the book, and she pushes it toward me. "Put it on the hall table as you go out."

CHAPTER FOURTEEN

The afternoon light is all but gone, and the bus home is crowded with commuters. My stomach is rumbling, but something tells me there's no dinner waiting for me. Chuck will still be at work. He's always at work. I get off the bus a stop early and walk in the gathering darkness to the funeral home.

Chuck is at his desk, flipping through a stack of paperwork, a bag of chips open beside him.

"Grab yourself a pop, Marlie. Did you bring some homework to do?"

Around a mouthful of his chips, I say, "I don't have any."

He tips back in his chair and puts his feet on the desk. Maybe he knows that I lie. He's reading my face.

"That girl and the train," he says. "You remember?"

"Annie."

"Yes. Annie. There's more to that story. I've never told anyone." Chuck pauses, looks like he's weighing whether or not he should tell me. "There was someone else there that day. Someone else who knows."

Chuck laces his fingers together, his knuckles white under the pudge.

"Who? You? You were there?"

"No. Mark wasn't my friend."

My mouth goes dry. "Sid."

Sid and Chuck took over the funeral parlor from their father. Sid wears a gray suit, sharply pressed each day, and combs his hair over his bald spot. He does the upstairs stuff. My mom calls him "serious." Severe. That's how I'd describe Chuck's brother, Sid.

Chuck nods his head. "He never told anyone. But Mark picked him up that morning. I heard his car. Mark's car only fired on five cylinders and you always knew when he'd arrived. But Sid came home alone, long after dark. His boots were wet and he didn't look anyone in the eye for months. Least of all me. It never even occurred to me to ask why."

"You never asked him? Not even later, when his pervert friend was arrested?"

Chuck is chewing on his lip. "No. Especially not then."

"Oh."

"I didn't want to hurt him. Sid and I, we're not close like you and Elliott. I mean, I love him, but I don't know what's important to him — maybe I don't even know him. But one thing I know, for years, and maybe even still, Sid was haunted."

Chuck is wringing his hands, his knuckles popping. I put my hands on his. "Maybe Sid didn't see anything. Maybe it had nothing to do with Annie's brother."

Chuck sighs and shakes his head. "Maybe I should have said something the day we buried her."

Seeing Chuck like this scares me. There's a quake in his voice.

"Sid's been paying. It's only these last couple of years since Mark was arrested that there's been any joy for Sid, in anything. Whatever he did or didn't do, I forgive him. I can't do anything but forgive him. For a while there, I thought he was next under the train. You know?"

I don't know. Not really. I don't know if I'll ever be able to forgive Dad for taking Elliott. For taking himself, removing himself so completely and permanently and irrevocably from my life.

I say to Chuck, "And whatever you did or didn't do, it was for Sid. Maybe you just need to forgive yourself."

Chuck smiles. "Sweet, simple Annie. There was no justice for her." His chin slumps to his chest.

I want to take Chuck's warm, round bulk and hug it to me. I want to hold him, like Mom holds Elliott when he strikes out three times in one game. But I don't. I'd like to say that I think Annie would forgive him, and Sid too, and probably even her slimy brother. Because it sounds like Annie was that kind of person.

I wonder what they'd do to her at James Last Secondary.

CHAPTER FIFTEEN

~~~

Ms. Grimshaw left the library today carrying a gym bag. Ms. Grimshaw is working out — I wonder if she wears those shiny tights and high-cut leotard things that make thighs look like hams. I'm happy to see her leave. I've been afraid she might say something about me being in her office yesterday.

I guess Mike got what he wanted from the computer. He hasn't been back in today, none of them have. Maybe he told them all that I'm too big a loser, that they should ignore me. Not that I care about Mike. I can't figure out what the others see in him. But with Ravin and Cor, it was like I had friends again.

That's why I jump up, practically falling all over myself, when Cor comes in.

"Hey, Cor."

"Hey."

"You finish the book? It was due yesterday, but I plugged in a renewal for you." I'm embarrassed I sound so eager. Cor is gazing around the library, like she's never really seen it before.

"I dumped Julian." Her voice sounds funny. Kind of thick.

"Oh." I'm not sure what to say. Sorry? Congratulations? Without Julian at her side, she seems to list a bit.

"I got a tongue stud." She sticks out her tongue to show me.

"Is it sore?"

"Actually, no." She IS talking differently. "The mouth is amazingly clean." She says, "amathingly." "My mom likes this one better than my nose stud, because she can't see it."

"Well, I think it's very nice. I mean, it looks good on you. In you. I mean . . ."

Cor laughs. "Yeah. Whatever. I'd go with you, you know, if you wanted to get one. Not a tongue stud, necessarily (Nethetharily). Maybe one for your ear."

I shudder. I don't have pierced ears for a reason. Mom did her own ears when she was fourteen, with a needle. One ear, I could almost see her doing. But the second, after she knew how much it was going to hurt?

"They use a gun thing. It goes in so fast you don't even feel it. You just have to keep it clean for a while. That's Mike's problem. He doesn't keep it clean. He got one here, you know?" She pats her chest. "It got infected. He could squeeze an inch of pus out of it, just like toothpaste."

Nice.

Cor wanders off down the shelves of fiction books, running her finger along the spines. "The guys had a good time with that one. Called him some interesting names." She pauses at a book and pulls it out. "This is in the wrong spot. Should I move it?"

"Sure. Go for it."

Cor slips it into place, straightening the spines neatly to the edge of the shelf. I grab a pile of paperbacks off the trolley. She takes them from me without saying a word and starts shelving. I get another pile for myself. We work alongside one another without speaking.

Then, she says, "I still really like him."

"Mike?"

"No. Julian."

"So why did you break up?" I glance at her, hoping I haven't asked more than I should have.

She sighs. "He'd do anything for me. Or Mike. That's his problem. He'll do anything for anybody. I used to like that he was so easygoing."

She's quiet for a long time, shelving books. I wait for her to tell me more. When she doesn't, I ask her, "Do you like Mike?"

She pauses and looks at me. "I've known him forever. He and his mom used to live in the complex behind my house. We ran through the sprinkler together. I've seen Mike naked, Marlie." She laughs. "Then when we were eight his mom remarried and got the big house they're in now."

"So he went to elementary school with Ravin?"

She shakes her head. "Nope. Went to live with his dad in Toronto. That lasted until about a year ago. I met up with him again last year in ninth grade."

"Troubles with his dad?"

She shrugs. "He never talks about it."

"He must be happy to be back with his mom."

"Happy?" With a decisive thump, she shelves a book. "I don't think I'd use that word."

It's hard to contemplate that Elliott might feel the same way, someday, that he could lose the sense of being his mother's son. I guess if he stayed away long enough, it could happen. Maybe it's already started. But Elliott isn't anything like Mike. A little snake of fear makes me shiver.

"Cor, why would Mike have a list of people's names? People he hates. Their addresses and stuff about their families?"

Her hand pauses on the spine of a book. She doesn't look at me.

"He might have my name on that list now," I say.

With the smallest shrug she says, "In a lot of ways, he's a very different guy." She shelves the last book, her hand lingering on the shelf. She's still not looking at me. "But you can go crazy trying to figure people out. Sometimes it's just better not to try." Her forehead furrows briefly, then she dusts off her hands and smooths the front of her black lacy top. She looks at me now and says, "I think I've just become a librarian's slave's slave." She laughs, and the little stud in her tongue clicks on her teeth.

✧ ✧ ✧

Ravin is waiting at my locker after school. "Hey, Marlie." She doesn't smile, but it feels friendly. I go with her down to the wood shop corridor. Cor is there and Mike, with two other guys. I don't remember them being at his party. Mike's face and shirt are coated in white powder, and he's grinning.

"You started a fire?" Cor is standing with her hands on her hips, glaring at Mike.

"Just a car fire. It doesn't really count." A look passes between Mike and Cor, and his grin changes to a smirk. "We got it out before the alarm went off."

"And before Mr. Gertz saw it." The two guys are laughing. Mr. Gertz teaches auto shop. He has absolutely no hair left.

Cor crosses her arms, her face flat and angry.

One of the guys is talking. "Some idiot brought his old Buick to the shop to get the brakes done. I'd never leave my car in a school shop. It's like asking for it to get trashed."

The other guy nods.

"Mike revved it up like it was the space shuttle." He's laughing. "Flames came pouring out of the engine. Then he revved it some more, to see what would happen. That's when we figured we better get the fire extinguisher."

The three of them are bent over laughing.

Ravin raises her voice above the laughter. "It's a good thing you didn't get caught."

"So what?" Mike says. "Fiona likes me. I'm the son she never had."

"Yeah, right."

"No, really. Remember the time I drove her beemer into the auto shop pit? She wasn't mad about that. Only because I tried to fix the dents."

"Yeah, BONDO." The guys are laughing again.

"What do you mean?" Mike says to them. "I did a great job. You couldn't hardly tell it'd been spray-bombed."

"Except that it wasn't the same color!"

"Close enough. Her standards are too high."

"Anyone else would have been suspended," Ravin sniffs. "Any one of us, anyway."

"That's right. Anyone else wouldn't have got her keys in the first place." Mike puts on an innocent face. "How about an oil change for your car, Mrs. Birk? And maybe a wash?"

The guys laugh.

One says, "You're like her 'positive reinforcement' program gone mutant."

"Like Frankenstein," the other one says.

"You even look like Frankenstein, with your face all white. Hey, FRANK."

Mike leans over the hallway fountain to wash his face. "What you don't realize is the special relationship I have with our principal. The 'understanding'." He splashes water over his face. "It's a relationship forged over many a detention. Our Mrs. Birk wants me to succeed. She'll do anything to help me succeed." Mike dries his face on his shirtsleeve. He's not smiling anymore. "And so I will."

They don't notice the kid standing at the end of the hall, listening. Big Lex from science. They don't see him turn quietly and retreat. They don't see his little round eyes turn to mine and hold me for an instant, as if to say "come away with me."

Cor does. She opens her mouth to say something, maybe to call the alarm. But she doesn't. She looks at me and slowly shakes her head. Don't say a word.

When I look back up the hall, Lex is gone.

CHAPTER SIXTEEN

The sound of funeral music filters down to Chuck's workroom. Saturday is a busy day here — Mom will sing at three funerals. Chuck has his clients carefully prepared and waiting. He's puttering now, stretching a gray wig over a Styrofoam head. He's painted the lips on the head a bright red.

I've done my nails, no polish, and am buffing them with a soft suede pad.

"You did a nice job on your nails."

"Thanks." I hold them out to admire their sheen. "Chuck, what did you look like when you were in high school?"

Chuck extends his arms out at his sides. "I've always looked like this. When I was fourteen, I looked like this." He's just about as wide as he is tall.

"You must have had more hair."

"Thank you for that. Yes. I had nice hair. It was my best feature, thick and wavy on top, slicked back over the ears. With my hair, I was a babe magnet."

"Yeah," I laugh, "you probably met lots of girls in the Junior Undertaker's Club."

"Pity there wasn't such a club. It should be offered as part of the curriculum, really. Schools could have undertaking shops right next to the food science kitchens."

"Were you really a babe magnet?"

Chuck busies himself at the wig. "Well, there was someone. For a while."

Chuck with a girlfriend. This was good. "Was she pretty?"

"Clarice. Eyes like a summer sea. Dark curls around her face. Clarice was beautiful, but she wasn't what you'd call pretty." Chuck turns the Styrofoam head to work on the back. "We met at Chess Club."

"Chess?" I snort.

"Chess is a noble game. You should try it."

"So what happened? With you and Clarice?"

Chuck winds some fat pink rollers into the wig. His fingers are the same color as the rollers. "She dumped me. After a year and a half, she dumped me for a guy named Mitch with a face Hollywood would love, who only wanted her because he hated me. To show me that he was something and I was nothing. He dumped Clarice a couple of months later."

"That's awful! Did you take her back?"

Chuck's hands pause in the gray wig. "No." He says it slowly, shaking his head. "That wasn't really an option. Clarice did some nasty things to me, in her brief reign with the beautiful people."

"Like?"

"Like, telling them things I'd told her. Things I'd never told anyone else. Mitch took great pleasure in the knowledge. Twisted me up like a wire tie. I think Clarice regretted it."

"But you couldn't forgive her."

"I tried. But I couldn't forget."

"And you never met anyone else?"

Chuck turns the wig, inspecting it front and back. "No." Then he turns to face me. "But I've never stopped looking."

My heart hurts for Chuck. He's a great guy. So what if he looks like a troll?

"Maybe you could teach me chess, sometime."

"What, like a mercy date?"

"For you or for me? Besides, Elliott would love it. I could teach him when he comes back. He'd pick it up in a flash."

It's a sure thing Dad isn't teaching him chess. Dad doesn't have that kind of concentration. Once he set Elliott's infant carrier on the top of the car, Elliott in it, as he helped me into my seatbelt. Then he got in behind the wheel. A woman with eyes the size of dinner plates honked her horn at him, and only then he remembered Elliott.

Or there's the playhouse he started building for me, the one we use now as a shed, even though it has no windows, doors, and only half the roof.

Or the jobs he decided he didn't like, after working for ten days.

Mom says Dad is impetuous, that he can only see miles ahead of himself, not the little steps it takes to get there.

Chuck watches me with wary eyes. "Elliott will beat us both. Probably the first time he plays."

"That would be good. I'd be happy."

"Yes. I would be too."

❖ ❖ ❖

Chess isn't as boring as I thought, although I play it poorly.

We're at the kitchen table. Supper has been cleared away. Mom is watching us play, although I can tell she's distracted. Sundays are the worst for her, without Elliott. Her eyes keep straying over to the phone. Eventually she wanders out of the room. Chuck is getting red in the face, playing with me. "Watch your center! You're too reckless."

I love the way the Queen sweeps across the board, all fire and passion. I'll risk the game just to see her move.

"Look how you've left yourself open," Chuck says, shaking his head. "Think before you move."

Chuck can ponder a move forever. "Trust your instincts," I say to him.

"Why did I teach you this game, a perfectly good and civil pastime, only to have you turn it into a bloodbath?"

"If you played this slowly with Clarice, I'm not surprised she dumped you."

"Marlena Peters, that is rude. Checkmate."

"I surrender to your superior skills, oh, master. I am unworthy and deserve to die."

Chuck scoops the chess pieces into a well-worn cardboard box. "You don't give yourself enough credit."

Ravin said the same thing once. "And you," I say to Chuck, "you hold the gold-card of self-esteem?"

"You think I have low self-esteem?"

"Maybe." Maybe, I think, that's why you won't make a play for Mom. "Maybe that's why I let you win at chess."

"You let me win?" Chuck dumps the chess pieces back out onto the table.

"I want to be white this time." I pick up the Queen. In

real life she'd wear a helmet and carry a broad sword.

"How did Clarice play? Was she shrewd and calculating, like you?"

"You flatter me. No, actually. She played like you. A mad fool."

"I like her better already." I plunk the Queen into position.

CHAPTER SEVENTEEN

~~~~

Mom is sitting at the kitchen table in her bathrobe, drinking coffee and reading the Wednesday morning paper. She looks up when I come in. Her eyes get big. Really big.

"What did you do to your hair?" Her chair scrapes back and she gets up, drawing the belt of her robe tighter around her. "Marlena, look at me."

I toss my pack on the counter and stand still for her inspection. The experiment last night wasn't, I admit, completely successful. The color was supposed to be "Mahogany Sunset," a glamorous shade of deep, shiny brown. On me, it looks orange.

Mom's hands are in my hair, tugging it so it stands straight off the scalp. I think of primates, grooming one another. Orangutans, maybe. "You washed it out, didn't you?"

"Yes, MOTHER. I followed the instructions exactly."

"Exactly?"

"Well, practically exactly. It said to leave it on for twenty minutes, but when it started frothing I got scared and washed it out."

Mom stands with her arms folded.

"And there was a tube of something left in the box, but I think it was just conditioner. Or something."

Mom's chin lifts at this. "Oh, Marlena, that was the stuff that gives the color!"

I brace myself for the lecture. But she hugs herself and starts to laugh. I can't remember the last time Mom laughed. For sure it hasn't been since Elliott left.

"What? It's not THAT bad." I check my reflection in the toaster. "It's just a little orange."

Mom pulls me into her arms. She seems fragile, like a bird, with hollow bones. Her breath smells like coffee.

"We could go to the salon," she says. "I don't work until 11:00. You could skip the morning and go to school after lunch." She looks at herself in the toaster. "I could use a trim, too."

Maybe if I don't breathe, if I don't move a muscle, even the little ones between my ribs, this moment won't disappear. Mom and me. We haven't really been alone together since Elliott was born. I feel guilty for thinking it, but it's true. Elliott occupied us both. He was our "glue."

"Sure, Mom, okay."

"I'll just throw on my clothes." Mom heads into her bedroom. She's still talking to me, her voice muffled as she rummages in the closet. "Maybe Gloria can do us. She's a wizard. Oh, it'll feel so good to have this hair out of my eyes."

I put some bread into the toaster and pour a glass of milk. I think I'll cut my hair, too. It just hangs at my chin doing nothing. Cor's hair is short. So is Ravin's. Not that Ravin would like us to look all the same.

"Getting the right hair color is tricky. I've done it, but it never looks the same as on the box." Mom's voice is cheerful, almost excited. "And, of course, the models they use have beautiful hair to begin with."

I butter my toast and eat it standing at the counter. I flip the switch off on Mom's coffeepot. "Like, why would anyone color perfect hair?" I call back.

Mom is coming down the hall, doing up the belt on her skirt. "Exactly," she says. "They should use real people on those packages. Truth in advertising . . ."

The phone rings. The sound ricochets in the kitchen. Mom's face goes gray and she runs for the phone. It rings again and she fumbles to pick it up.

"Hello? Elliott?" Silence. "Elliott, is that you, honey? Elliott!"

Her hands are shaking as she lowers the phone. "A hang-up." She punches the special code the police gave her to trace the call.

"Elliott wouldn't phone then just hang up," I say.

"Hello, Operator. Were you able to trace that call? It's Elizabeth Peters. Yes, thank you. I'll hold."

"Neither would Dad. Once he decides to do something, he does it. It was probably a wrong number."

Mom is standing with one arm crossed over her chest, chewing on her thumb.

"It wasn't Elliott, Mom. It was just a wrong number."

"Yes, I'm still here. No, I'll keep holding."

"Mom?" No answer.

I slide my pack off the counter. Now I'm going to have to run or be late. Mom is looking at the floor. "Well, I'm going to go to school. Okay?" Nothing.

The kitchen door bangs closed behind me.

Anyway, I like my hair orange. What's the big deal?

⬥ ⬥ ⬥

Cor catches me at second period outside the gym. "Hey. I love that hair color." She oohs and aahs while I tell her how it came to be. "No, it looks great. Way better than brown."

Cor's hair is different every week. Today it's something between purple and burgundy.

"I'll come see you at lunch," she says. "I need a new book."

I wave goodbye. Mike is just going into gym. His shirt is out of his shorts, and he's wearing black socks with his black Velcro shoes.

"Tape your rings," I hear Coach Schroeder holler.

"Hey, Marlie." It's Cor. "This weekend we could do our hair together. If you want to."

I smile, relieved to think I won't always have orange hair. "Yeah, Cor. I want to."

CHAPTER EIGHTEEN

—nn—

"What clown rode their bike today?"

After Monday classes, Cor and I are coming down the steps out of the back door of the school. It's been snowing since last night, erasing the line between November and December with heavy fat flakes. The lone bike, carefully locked in the rack, is covered in a white blanket.

I love the first snow. It would make me sing, if I was a singer. I think snow is Mother Nature's perfect precipitation. All the colors and all the light of the entire world is in an untracked field of snow.

Elliott would love this. He'd be pulling on last year's snow pants and finding gloves and boots and heading for the big hill with his sled. He and McLean would spend hours in the snow, until they were so cold they couldn't form words. Then they'd sit at the kitchen table with hot chocolate, their noses running and their cheeks red, eating mini-marshmallows one by one.

I hope wherever Elliott is, he's got snow.

"I made Honor Roll."

I'm jarred from my thoughts. It doesn't surprise me.

Last weekend I went to Cor's and she helped me with a poetry assignment. And my hair. She made both look easy.

"First time in this school. Last year was a write off."

I watch her closely. What did Mike mean, exactly, that day in the library when he said, "Ask Cor"? Now doesn't seem to be the time to ask.

"I've never been anywhere close to honors."

"Well, yeah. I mean, you have to study. And actually turn in assignments."

I squirm at this. I'd told Cor that I turned in my social studies assignment late and lost a full letter grade.

"Does your mom give you money for making Honor Roll?"

Cor gives me a quick look. "Or a sport-utility vehicle? Not likely. No, Honor Roll is my way out. I need a scholarship. Come on. My feet are freezing."

Mine are too. But I don't care. I take a deep breath of new winter air.

"Did you ever make snow angels?"

Cor shoves me off the path into the snow. "Of course. Everyone makes snow angels."

I step back onto the path and shake the snow off my pants. "Do you think Ravin has ever made a snow angel?"

"Well, okay, everyone EXCEPT Ravin." Cor laughs. "Ravin wouldn't like the concept."

"Of angels?" An image of Ravin sitting in Sunday school makes me want to laugh.

"What I meant was, she wouldn't like the idea of being on the ground."

"Even in the snow?" If I could be absolutely sure no one would see me, I'd make an angel right here and now.

Cor shook her head. "It's about control, or freedom, or some combination of the two. I'm sure that's why she skated. Just razor edges between her and the earth, edges that cut gravity away like wire through clay. On skates she could free herself completely."

I jump lightly in place, loving the crunch of the snow under my feet. "So what does she do now to free herself, since she's not skating?"

Cor buries her hands in her pockets, hunching her shoulders against the cold. "She frees us."

"From what?" I'm puffing small white clouds as I jump.

"From ourselves."

I stop jumping.

She continues. "Really, when you think about it, that's what Ravin does. She makes us think we're not victims. And then we're not."

"What about Nevkeet? When something so awful happens, do you ever stop being a victim?"

Her eyebrows lift. "Nevkeet? Maybe he just tripped."

I laugh, but she doesn't. The laughter dies in my throat. "But Mike saw."

"He says he did."

"Cor!"

Now she laughs. "You look as white as the snow. I'm joking, of course!"

I don't know whether to laugh or not. I stand at the bike rack, the snow melting inside the back of my collar, the afternoon light already flattening over the playing field, dulling the snow to gray.

"Anyway, Ravin likes to win. And so long as there's a good battle to be fought, then Ravin is in control." Cor shivers. She's wearing the same light jacket that she's worn all fall. "Okay, let's walk already."

Then she stops. "Wait a minute." She picks her way to the bike rack and kicks the lone bike. The snow showers off in a whisper.

"I knew it!" she whoops. "It's Julian's! It's the bike he thought got stolen last spring. He must have put it in this rack instead of the one he always uses, then forgot. He wouldn't have even noticed it here, with other bikes in the rack." She laughs and shakes her head. "Poor Julian."

"Are you going to tell him?"

"No. I like it where it is." She returns to the path and slips her arm through mine, for warmth. "It reminds me of a monument, all alone in the rack."

"Like The Tomb of the Unknown Student."

"Yeah. Or victim, maybe."

"Cor, did you ever skate?"

"Just on hand-me-down hockey skates. How about you?"

Our feet scrunch on the snow. "Are you kidding? Although I did have an ice show Barbie who did quite well in competition. The judges loved her, even the snotty ones. She always got perfect marks."

"That Barbie. Hers is a perfect world."

The snow feels too good to just go home. I leave Cor at her house and continue on to the funeral home. By the time I get there, I'm happy for the warmth of the building. As I walk down the hall, I can see that the lights are off in Chuck's workroom, but light from the windows at street level allows me to see in the open door.

Chuck's table is covered in a white sheet, some rounded form on it waiting for him. I click on the light and pull a stool up beside the table.

Chuck used to pick up Elliott and me from school sometimes when Mom was working. He drives old funeral cars. The ones the family rides in. You always get looks when you drive with Chuck. Elliott and I would go out to the loading loop, where all the moms waited in their minivans, and there would be Chuck in his long black car. The other kids would squeal and point. "Look, it's a funeral car!" Even the parents gave Chuck's car a wide berth, like they might catch something from it. Like grief.

One time Chuck picked us up and said, "You'll have to ride up front today." He had a car the length of a football field and we were supposed to sit up front.

"Why?" Elliott asked.

"Never mind why. Just get in the front."

"You have somebody back there, don't ya?" Elliott tried to peer through the darkened glass.

"Just get in." Chuck opened the front door and shoved us in.

Elliott was craning his neck over the back of the seat. "He does! Look, Marlie."

Sure enough, there in the back was a big black body bag.

"Mom isn't going to like this."

"Just shush about the bag. It's all sealed up."

Elliott pushed the button to open his window. "Hey, Josh," he yelled. "There's a dead body in the back seat."

Josh's mother grabbed his hand and yanked him to their

car.

"Elliott, do up that window." Chuck turned to me. "It's a last minute job. I had to pick it up on the way over."

"Hey, Alex, we got a dead body . . ."

I grabbed Elliott and anchored him onto the seat. It's amazing I ever had any friends.

When I look at the shape under the sheet on the table, it almost looks like it's breathing. I open my pack and pull out my science term assignment. Mr. Inkster's given us a choice: growing fruit flies, exploring the reproductive cycle of mushrooms, or something involving crystals and Bunsen burners. Larvae, spores, or combustible fuel. All of these seriously bore me.

The form under the sheet *is* breathing, I'm sure of it. Oh this is good, I think to myself. It's like the stories Keely and I used to tell at sleepovers, about the guy who is buried alive by accident, and when the family discovers their mistake and dig him up, he's got his hand stuffed down his throat to suffocate himself.

With my pencil, I reach over and poke the form.

It sits up.

"EEEK!" I shriek.

"AAAGH!" The sheet falls away. Chuck is clutching his heart. "You scared me half to death. Don't you ever knock?"

"I scared YOU? What were you doing under the sheet? And why would I knock if there was just a corpse in here?"

Chuck slides off the table, tugging his lab coat down over his big butt. "I needed to rest my eyes." We both gather our breath in a sigh, look at one another, then break out laughing. Chuck notices my paper. "What's that you've got there?"

I pass him the science assignment. He reads it. "These sure haven't changed much. I think I did the same one."

"Do you still have it?" I say, batting my eyes.

"Like I'd give it to you. You should do this one, with the Bunsen burner. It looks like the most interesting."

"You mean it looks like the lesser of three evils."

"No, you'll like it. You hold different stuff in the flame, and it turns colors. Then you figure out why."

"I'd like to figure out why I have to do it."

Chuck slaps me on the head with the paper. "So you can go to college and study something that really interests you."

"I don't think I'm exactly college material."

"Based on what?"

"Oh, I don't know. Maybe my marks."

"So change them."

I think of Mike and the school computer.

"Study. Work harder. Bring your homework here to do it. I'll crack the whip."

He would, too.

"I loved college. All through high school they called me Maggot and stole my lunch money, but in college no one cares. The jocks and the preps and the rest of us, suddenly we're all the same. Your dad loved it too."

"Dad went to college?"

"Well, yeah, for a short while. Then he met your mom. And then there was you. But he was in Engineering. That's not easy to get into. He used to take me to their parties. They'd wait until the washrooms in the Arts building were busy, then they'd switch the signs for Men and Women. One time they took the handles off the inside of the doors, so when you were in the washroom, you couldn't get out."

He giggles thinking about it.

"So what did you study? Advanced refrigeration?"

"Very funny. I studied Latin, the dead language." Chuck tosses the assignment in front of me. "Bunsen burners, Marlie. Trust me on that."

CHAPTER NINETEEN

～～～

METAL DEATH
by Marlie Peters

Bang bang, you're dead.
I just shot you in the head.
Don't get up, 'cause it's no game.
You're the one. I had your name.
Cylinder, missile, teeny tiny stud.
Metal infiltrator,
Domin, penen, disintegrator.
Dissolve you, like fear, like discontent,
Like a nothing, used-up friend.
You're magic marker
Little black dots,
A drop of red.
Bang bang, you're dead.

It's going to be a long Wednesday. Mr. Bates is sitting on the arm of his chair, his hands folded over one knee, a look of concern on his face. A sheet of loose-leaf paper hangs from his folded hands. The nine o'clock bell just rang — he intercepted me at homeroom.

"Mrs. Pincott showed me your poem, Marlie."

I can see her red ink on the sheet of paper he's holding. It's the poem Cor helped me with.

"What did I get?"

Mr. Bates looks at the paper. "Mrs. Pincott hasn't graded it yet. She has some concerns about the subject matter."

"She said we could write about anything we wanted."

Mr. Bates levels his gaze at me. "And what is it that you're writing about?"

I take the paper from him. "You can't tell from reading it?"

With a careful sigh, he says, "What the poem says to me is the writer might be in some kind of trouble. That she's calling out for help."

I level my stare back at him. "It's just a poem." I toss it on his desk. A stupid poem I had to write for an even more stupid English class.

He seems to ignore this. "And maybe someone is doing something that frightens you."

I don't like how he knows this. I get up and shove the chair backward, out of my way.

"It's just a poem," I repeat. Hardly even mine, really, Cor helped me with it so much. She said it was about piercing. Not that I'm going to tell Mr. Bates that Cor practically wrote the assignment for me. I turn to leave his office.

"Maybe you need to talk to someone. Your mother, perhaps?"

I spin to face him. "Mom is a little preoccupied. Elliott's been missing for five weeks now." My voice is too loud, but I don't care. "And you have to have something to talk about, in order to talk, right? I can take care of myself." I push open his door and let it slam behind me.

☙ ☙ ☙

Cor stands with me in the main hall just after the last bell. An aromatic class of twelfth-grade boys is leaving the gym, their running shoes squealing on the tile floor. Several stop to read a poster being hung by two giggling girls in almost identical sweaters.

When the crowd clears, Cor and I move over to read it, too.

"The Black and White, December 15th. The annual Christmas dance," Cor says. "Fancy. Everyone goes."

I look at the poster. It's been screened in black on white paper. A border of black holly and jingle bells runs along the bottom.

"So you wear black or white, I guess."

"Oh yeah." Cor rolls her eyes. "Some people go all out — tuxedos, gowns, even limos."

I point to the date. "It's only a couple of weeks away."

"It's always the weekend before classes finish. People will have been planning for it since September." She pauses, then adds, "I'm sure that Mike has."

A dance. Of course that would mean a dress, or nice pants, anyway. I wonder if I own anything that qualifies as "fancy," not counting the larvae costume from Cousin Myron's wedding. Not that I plan on going. Cor and I start walking toward the back doors of the school. The gym hallway is like a gauntlet, kids lining it both sides, tracksuits and team uniforms and logo shirts, and about a million dollars' worth of the best running shoes. Up ahead, I see the familiar clump of girls' volleyball suits and Keely's blonde pony. Keely would have known about this dance. She's probably been shopping every weekend for just the right dress. Shopping with Loren.

Cor lays a gentle hand on my arm. "It's too crowded. Let's turn around and go the long way."

"No. We can use this hallway." My fingers tighten into fists, thinking about Loren and the locker room. "We have just as much right to be here as they do."

Cor hesitates.

I say, "You don't have to go this way. But I am."

She turns toward the hall and takes a deep breath. It is a long corridor, and there must be a hundred kids in it. "Okay," she says. "All for one."

A few of the older girls roll their eyes as we walk by them. One guy spits into the fountain. I keep my elbow just touching Cor's, my eyes forward. I won't look down. My breath is quick, my arms and legs feel rubbery. The hallway sounds are muffled by the sound of my heart in my ears.

Two boys a year ahead of me fall into step with Cor, making faces and rude suggestions. Almost imperceptibly, she moves in closer to me. A group of three girls are lobbing friendly insults at some boys. As we pass, they stop talking, then I hear them laughing behind us. The noise in the hall is starting to swirl, a vortex of alien voices, with Cor and me at its center.

Their faces blend, the edges between them fade. They are nameless — just "them." It's not all of them, I know that. But it feels like every person in that hallway would like to see us fall.

The blonde pony turns, and Keely registers a quick moment of recognition. It's her eyes I hold, my vision an iron cable from Cor and me to them. She looks away, laughing. But when she feels my stare, she looks back at me.

A hand comes out and knocks the pack off my shoulder onto my arm. I ignore it. The boys beside Cor are making animal noises, thrusting their hips, their faces lit with excitement. I ignore them, too. My focus is on Keely.

Her friends are watching us, laughing, their hands around their faces, their shoulders touching. Keely is still, her eyes at first derisive, now widening, in fear.

Cor follows my stare. "It's okay, Marlie." Her hand comes up to my arm. "We're almost through."

We've had to weave our way through the crowded hallway, squeezing past boys a foot taller than us, past girls who set their heels and won't move an inch to let us by. With my stare locked on Keely, I stop. Cor falters, but just for an instant. She moves back beside me, her chin high, her eyes impassive. The girls clustered around Keely titter, their laughter less sure, their faces showing small uncertainty. And Keely looks down.

In that crystal instant, the balance shifts for Cor and me. The voices recede, the boys step back, and, slowly, like a February icicle, the crowd in the hall melts away to let us pass.

Behind us, the knots and clusters form again, like we hadn't even been there.

Keely's blonde pony turns as I pass, and I feel her watching me, her fear dissolving, the contempt again lining her face.

Beside me, Cor is breathing again, her shoulders relaxing, her steps more sure. At the door she looks at me, just long enough to connect, then she lifts her chin again, and we push through the doors and go outside.

"I don't much care for dances," I say.

"No," she says. "Neither do I."

CHAPTER TWENTY

"Maybe I should go to the dance. I could sing some of my old Nashville numbers."

Mom whines out the lyrics to an ancient folk song. She seems happier tonight. Maybe because Chuck has brought our favorite Friday night supper: pizza.

"Mom, please. Think of my brain cells."

For the last couple of days, everyone in the school has been talking about the Black and White dance: what they'll wear, their hair, who's going with who. Half the earth could slip into the ocean and this school wouldn't know about it. But they know whose parents will likely chaperone the Black and White, that so-and-so is wearing her sister's dress from last year (gasp!), and that Mr. Bates the guidance counselor is NOT going to play his guitar this year. He's promised.

"Very funny. Or something from the top forty of funeral songs."

Chuck leans back on the kitchen chair. When he does this, his feet swing like a little kid's.

"Still no vegetables?" I say to him, eyeing the pizza.

He sets his chair down with a thump and picks at some tiny green specks under the cheese. "Green pepper. See?"

"It might be green pepper. But then again, have you seen the people who work in the pizza shop? It could be almost anything."

"Marlena." Mom's warning voice. "You are a sweetie, Chuck, for bringing this for us. You don't have to take care of us, you know."

"Yes, he does," I say. "Unless you were planning on peanut butter and pickles again."

Mom gets quiet. She found out who it was who called and then hung up. It was a telephone solicitor, hoping we wanted to get our rugs cleaned. Chuck gives me the "that's enough" look.

"What is your favorite funeral song?" Chuck asks Mom. Only at this kitchen table would funerals be a topic to cheer up somebody.

Mom smiles at him. "Well, there's always something new on the radio that works for funerals. Those are fun to sing. But my favorite is an old one, 'Amazing Grace.'"

That's my favorite too. When Mom sings that one you feel the skin lifting right off you.

"Sometimes," Mom is saying, "the room can be hard. No one will have cried the whole service. You wonder why they even came. Or it's one of those funerals where no one cares about the deceased — his or her name is just plugged into a standard eulogy like so much junk mail." Mom shakes her hair over her shoulders. "Then I sing 'Amazing Grace.' And they cry. It works every time."

Chuck laughs. "Your mom's funerals, they're always a two-tissue affair."

Mom sets a slice of pizza on her plate and incises it into tiny squares with her knife and fork. "People need to cry. Just like they need to laugh. That's why I'm there. Sometimes, afterward, at the tea, an old guy will look at me with watery eyes and take my hand and just hold it."

"Yeah," Chuck says. "He's got six years' worth of spots on his tie and he can't see over the steering wheel but he still knows a sweet young thing when he sees one."

"Chuck!"

Chuck isn't eating any pizza. He's sitting looking at Mom.

"So, you think I should sing 'Amazing Grace' at the school dance?"

"Now that would be something to see." Chuck crosses his hands over his belly.

"Don't even think about chaperoning the dance," I say. "Not that Mr. Bates would ask you. He hasn't called you, has he?"

"No," Mom replies.

"So you're not going."

They both look at me. "Oh?" says my mother.

"No, I mean it. Mr. Bates has more parents than he knows what to do with. He made an announcement today. 'No More Parents.' Really."

Chuck looks at Mom, and she at him. "Hmm," they both say.

CHAPTER TWENTY-ONE

Monday dawns pale gray. I stay in my bed, gathering myself for the week, listening to the chickadees. There must be ten of them in the tree outside my room, up at the crack of early, ready to defend their territory against all comers. Little feathered commandos. Then they stop singing. All at once.

How do they know to stop, all at the same time? Not one peep out of place, they stop on cue, instantly, and not one bird misses the signal. It's like they have a code or something, some pact of communication, that the very instant one bird stops, the others will too. Never mind that they're competing for the same bugs and the best branches. When one of them stops singing, that's it, no more singing.

I wish I'd asked Cor what she meant when she said that Mike had been planning for this dance. Not his dance steps, that's for sure. What if Mom is really serious about going?

I won't be able to see Cor at the library, either. I'll be spending lunch hour in the chem lab, working on my science project. Lex Lemley is doing the Bunsen burner experiment, too, and looks way too happy that I'm there. He always brings a huge lunch and sits close to me, even though the lab is practically empty. He did this project last year, so he knows what's supposed to happen, which is good. I don't have a clue. Mr. Inkster sits at his desk, eating wiggly things with chopsticks, dipping them in disgusting green paste. He reads paperback novels with cowboys on the cover and keeps the fire extinguisher right by his side.

☆ ☆ ☆

Mike and two of his friends are making their way through the crowded hallway. The last class before lunch has just finished, and there are kids at their lockers, others trying to get to theirs. I wind my way through the crowd and manage to grab Mike by the arm.

He spins, his face hard and angry, ready to fight back. When he sees it's me, he looks almost disappointed.

"Uh, I need to ask you about something. About the dance."

He yanks his arm away. "Not here you don't." He turns back down the hall.

I scramble to keep up with him. "Yeah, I do, Mike. It's really important."

He doesn't even turn to respond. "Not important enough."

I tug at his arm again. "Yes, it is. My mom is talking about going. And Chuck. And I'm just wondering if you're planning to do something."

He stops then, right in the middle of the hallway, and turns and faces me. The ring over his left eyebrow is imbedded in an oozy worm of red. His eyes are black slate. Sweat prickles under my collar and I drop my hand from his arm.

His voice hisses like steam. "Do you really think it makes any difference that your mommy and the grave digger might be at the dance?" He snorts. "That just makes it more interesting."

The breath catches in my throat, and suddenly I can see that list of his, with my mother's and Chuck's name on it. "Then you're making a mistake." The words come out more firmly than I meant.

He looks at the two guys with him, then back to me. His eyes narrow and his lips tighten and his words are made of steel. "What did you say?"

Now the sweat cools instantly to a chill. I wish Ravin was here, or Cor. I swallow hard and stutter, "I didn't mean anything by that. Just your ring." I motion to his eyebrow. "You're not turning your ring."

The two guys laugh. I bet they're thinking of his other ring. Relieved, and encouraged by their laughter, I add, "Everyone knows to turn their rings, Mike."

Mike flicks the hair off his face. He looks irritated by the laughter.

I blurt out, "And another thing. I've read that if a ring gets infected like that, if it gets rejected? Then it'll always be rejected."

That was probably going too far. He silences the sniggering of the guys with one leaden look and locks me in his glare. "Well, if anyone knows about rejection, it would be you. Your old man didn't even want you."

With that he turns his back on me, shouldering a boy angrily out of his way. The guy stumbles, knocking into me.

I stand there, dumbly, still smarting from Mike's remark.

"Who do you think you guys are?" the boy says.

Mike gives him the finger, then he and the other two disappear down the hall. A small crowd is gathering. I'm acutely aware of being alone.

The boy turns to me. "You guys are mutants. You should be locked up. You're jerks. Freakin' jerks."

The crowd is tightening.

I can feel the blood rushing to my face. The crowd is knotting around me, everyone pushing to get a better look. Breathing is useless — it's like the air isn't any good, and I have to stop myself from gasping. The guy is smiling, he knows he has me, but he's going to let me go. He's made his point. He turns slightly, to let me get out. I move for the opening, my eyes fixed on the tiny space in the crowd. Then someone's hands are on me, shoving me from behind. My head snaps back from the force. Desperately, I try to keep my footing. The only thing between me and the metal lockers is the guy. He's just turning away from me when I ram into him, my shoulder catching him under his rib cage. The breath goes out of him in a whoosh, just before his face hits the corner of a locker.

I want to say that I'm sorry. The guy is holding the side of his face, trying not to cry. They're calling me names now, nasty names, their voices angry. They don't know, or they don't care, that I stumbled. I push through the crowd. The guy's face is red and swollen, and he's looking at me with pure hate in his eyes.

❧ ❧ ❧

In the washroom next to the science lab I wash my face and collect myself. When I go in to the lab, Lex is already there, his books open and notebook ready. He's unpacking his lunch, and it smells wonderful. My mouth is actually watering. I pull out my peanut butter on plain white bread, eyeing the wrapper Lex is unfolding next to me. It's a sandwich made on a crusty brown loaf, with little seeds scattered over the crust.

"It's meatloaf. Want some of it?"

Lex's voice shocks me. I don't think I've heard him more than grunt all year. It's a deep voice, like a radio announcer.

"Ah, no, that's okay." He's looking at me, his squinty little eyes looking wet and pink. "But thanks."

"I've got two." He pulls out another wrapper from his pack. The aroma is of mustard and mayo and just the tiniest bit of onion.

I am without shame. "Okay, then. Thanks." I take the sandwich from him. I don't even wait for him to unwrap his. I just bite into it. The crust is firm, but not tough, and the filling is like nothing I've ever tasted. I take another bite, willing myself to slow down. "This is so good."

Lex smiles with his shiny lips. He bites into his sandwich with surprising delicacy, blotting his mouth with a paper napkin. I swallow my huge mouthful and brush the crumbs off my face.

"I make them in the morning, on frozen bread. So they're fresh."

"YOU made these?" I ask around another enormous bite.

"Well, it's my mom's meatloaf, but I made the sandwiches."

I look at Lex, trying to imagine him in a kitchen. With a mother. Maybe he was adopted.

"This one isn't my favorite, really. I make a chicken salad with avocado on sourdough that's better, I think."

"Mmm. I LOVE chicken salad. My dad used to make it with pecans."

"Did he toast them first?"

"The pecans? I have no idea."

"I toast them. It makes all the difference."

Mr. Inkster is looking over from his desk, the latest cowboy adventure open in front of him. A small blob of green paste is poised on the chopsticks he holds. His eyeglasses bob as he chews a mouthful of his lunch. It takes him a long time. Maybe it's squid. I tried squid, once. It was like eating rubber bands.

"You have to remember to illustrate it." Lex is talking to me.

"Huh?"

"Your term assignment. You have to include photos or illustrations. I know, from last year." He's squinting at the assignment sheet, a shiny knot in his forehead, his eyes even smaller with the strain of reading the sheet.

I look at Lex, his huge square hands on his sandwich, his short hair the same color as his scalp, his shoulders that come up around his ears. He's like one of those commercials, where a little kid has an adult voice.

"Let me read this through." I take the paper from him and hold it out in front. "I've got to read it out loud. This stuff never makes any sense to me."

I read it aloud, nice and slow, just like when I used to read to Elliott. Lex follows along, the knot in his forehead gradually easing. I ask him about stuff I don't get, and he explains how to do it. He's memorizing the steps, I'm sure of it. From his blue T-shirt comes the smallest whiff of fabric softener.

When I used to read to Elliott, at bedtime, his toes would curl and uncurl under the blanket, like a cat when you pat it.

"So," I say, handing Lex back the sheet. "What are you bringing for lunch tomorrow?" I'm joking, but he looks up, thinking about it.

"Chicken salad, I think. Yeah, chicken salad."

CHAPTER TWENTY-TWO

~~~

On Tuesday, the snow is all but gone and the sun is watery warm. In the yellow grass around the school, puddled melt water gleams weakly. Cor is propped on the bike rack, eating her breakfast — a bag of chips. Behind her in the schoolyard, people mill around, waiting until the last minute before going in to classes.

Cor turns and sweeps her arm over the scene. "It looks so normal, what you can see from here." She's talking without looking at me. "Like nothing strange or scary ever happens." She eats the chips, snipping small bites out of each one. "It's like one of those funguses, that has roots bigger than a redwood tree. The real stuff happens where no one can see it."

Elliott used to say that about the night. He asked me once how we really knew that our dreams were dreams. Maybe, he said, our real lives happen when we're asleep. So that night he tried to stay awake. He kept all the lights on in his room and sat up in his bed. He fell asleep face first at the foot of his bed, his legs still crossed.

Something in Cor's voice makes me ask, "What

happened to you?"

Cor looks at me, her eyes blank. "What are you talking about?"

"Last year. Why did you say it was a write-off?"

Cor turns her gaze again to the field. Her voice is flat, like she's reading. "I missed some school." She crumples the chip bag and jams it in her pocket.

"Because?" I prompt.

"Because I had a broken arm." She clicks her tongue stud on her teeth. "And some cracked ribs. And some other stuff."

I suck in a breath. "A car wreck?"

"No. I got beat up."

Just the way she says it makes my stomach roll, and I remember Mike in the library. *Ask Cor* . . . I swallow acrid spit. "Who did it, Cor?"

She jerks her head, indicating the schoolyard.

I follow her gaze out to the sea of people.

Her voice is sharp. "It's not like one person is guilty, or three, or ten. It's that it even happened. It might as well have been them all."

"And you're still here?" I hate myself for saying it. It's not like Cor has a lot of options open to her.

Cor looks at me. "Well, at least I know who the enemy is."

"Does Ravin know what happened?"

Cor shrugs. "I didn't know her before. I knew Mike. He was with me. Maybe she knew me. I doubt it. When I came back to classes last winter he'd already hooked up with Ravin. I just went along. And then Julian and I started going out. And it was just easier to stay than to leave."

"Mike was with you?"

She looks down at the ground. "We were having a big argument. Apparently they heard us, a bunch of older kids, out for laughs. Mike ran for help."

"They got away with it?"

"Of course. No one talked. Except for my black eyes and bandages, it was like it didn't even happen."

"I know he's an old friend of yours, but maybe Mike should have stayed and fought."

"Old friends? There are no old friends." I can hardly be surprised at the bitterness in her words. Cor steps down from the bike rack. "Someone gets sacrificed, me, Mike, you, them. It's all the same. We're all the same. No one knows anything about anyone else. Maybe there are no friends at all." She shoulders her pack and starts heading for the door. I follow her.

"Anyway, I didn't see a thing. The first blow came from behind and knocked me out."

"You were lucky they didn't kill you."

"Yeah," she says. "Maybe."

✧ ✧ ✧

The Bunsen burner breathes blue fire as Lex moves the forceps through the flame.

"Got it!" The camera I've borrowed from Mom whirs as the film advances. "I hope these turn out."

Lex is making notes. I don't know how he reads what he's written. The pen all but disappears in his great pink paw. And his spelling is awful.

He shared his lunch with me again. I should buy him a pop or something.

"I'll take these after school to get them developed and bring your copies tomorrow. That should just about wrap up the assignment."

Lex is bent over his notebook, his nose two inches from the paper. I'm not sure he even heard me. I load my text and papers into my backpack and flip it onto my shoulder.

"Marlie?" He's not looking at me.

"Yeah?"

"Thanks."

What the heck for, I'm thinking to myself. He was the one who figured out the assignment. Who knew what was supposed to happen. Who could explain it so it made sense. "No problem." I turn to the door.

"Marlie?"

"Yeah?"

"Mike is bad news."

I stop, the hairs lifting on the back of my neck. I turn slowly to face him. He's still bent over the notebook, but he's watching me, his tiny pink eyes looking needy.

My voice is harder than I mean it to be. "What are you talking about?"

Lex looks back down at his notebook. I wish I'd never eaten his sandwiches. Then I wouldn't have to listen to him. I could just turn my back on him, ignore him, pretend I didn't hear him. Or pretend that I didn't care. Or pretend that I don't already know that Mike is bad news.

"I don't like how he treats people."

"You don't like how he treats people!" I laugh. "You're the one with the monster-fists. You're the one who practically attacked him." I imitate the guys in science class. "'Get 'im, Lex. Sic 'im.'"

117

"I don't like how they treat people, either."

"So you're not like your friends, I suppose."

"They're not my friends, Marlie. Friends don't use you for their dirty work, then make fun of you behind your back."

His great big head droops on his neck. I pull out the chair beside him and plunk down. I'd like to put my hand on his shoulder.

"I'm sorry, Lex. I just assumed that you were part of their group."

"No." His head rolls back and forth. "I play football. Some of them play football. It doesn't mean that just because you play football you're an idiot."

"Okay, Lex. I said I was sorry."

He's breathing hard, his eyes bright. "Can't you see that Mike is doing the same thing to you? Mike is no one's friend. I've seen him laugh when he sticks a frog. And I've seen other stuff, too. He can joke with a teacher, be all charming and nice, and then cut her tires at lunch. Just because he can."

Maybe Mike did turn the microwave on for at least a second or two, with Ravin's cat inside.

Lex isn't looking at me anymore. His hands are folded together on top of his notebook, almost like he's praying. His massive head is swaying slowly from side to side.

"He's hurt people. And maybe I'm no better, because I've hurt people too. But as bad as I am, or as stupid, or as big a loser, nothing could make me beat people, beat and kick and punch people, people who've done nothing to me."

I think of Cor's face this morning when she was telling

me about what happened to her, how her face closed up, and the flatness of her eyes. His face has the same shuttered stillness. Now I do touch his shoulder, briefly. His eyes flick to mine, then back to the table. "What are you telling me?"

For a minute he doesn't move, like he hasn't heard me, like he isn't even breathing. Then he's standing up, his chair pushed back so suddenly that it clatters to the floor. Mr. Inkster starts, then eyes us sternly. Lex grabs his notebook and crams it in his pack.

"Lex." I try to get up but he shoves past me to the door. Without turning he speaks.

"Forget it. Just forget I said anything." Then he's gone.

CHAPTER TWENTY-THREE

—⌇—

Mom corners me at the sink after supper.

"Elaine talked to me today." Elaine is Keely and McLean's mother. "Keely has been telling her some disturbing stories about school."

My hands are in the soapy water, and I make like I'm scrubbing a pan in earnest.

"She says that some of the students are becoming quite aggressive. She says that kids are getting hurt." Mom's tone is half "I need some information," half "I need to be reassured."

I think about the kid I knocked into the locker and blood creeps up my face.

"The halls are crowded. Sometimes people push."

I can feel her watching me. I scrub at an imaginary spot on the pan.

"So you're not seeing anything of Keely." Mom knows about our falling-out. It's not a question.

I shake my head. "She's friends with Loren."

"Ah." Mom knows about Loren, too. "But you have some friends at school?"

I steal a quick glance at her. How much had Keely told her mother? "Sure. Yeah."

"Anyone I know?"

I lock my gaze on the pan in the sink. "I don't think so."

She stands beside me, her fingers at the collar of her sweater. "You could invite them over here. I'd like to meet them."

She doesn't deserve it, and I feel awful for doing it, but I laugh. "They're just some people at school. I don't know them that well." Not old friends, like Cor says, maybe not friends at all.

She takes the pan from me and rinses it under the tap, then reaches around me for a towel. "It takes awhile to get to really know people."

"Like Keely, for example?" Or Dad. I yank the plug out of the sink.

She dries the pan as carefully as I've washed it. "People change. Something happens in their life or doesn't happen." Her voice trails off.

Of course she's changed — and so have I. Losing Elliott happened. Tears smart at my eyes.

She sets the pan down and rests her hand on my arm. "All you can do is trust your instincts. And do what's right. Always the two things together."

I wish I could tell her about Nevkeet and Mike. That it's getting too complicated. That I'm afraid I'm getting in too deep. But then she checks the phone to see that it's plugged in, something she does about nineteen times everyday, and I know Mom is dealing with all she can right now.

❖ ❖ ❖

The next morning, as I go down the hall toward Cor's locker, I hear the sound of a boot slamming against metal, then Ravin's voice. "He is out of control."

Cor and Ravin don't even look at me when I walk up. Cor is avoiding Ravin's glare. She looks at me quickly, then down again at the floor. Ravin is chewing on a thumbnail, her brows an angry knot over her eyes.

"What's going on?" I say.

Ravin looks atomic. "Mike. That's what's wrong. He's planning something for the dance."

"The Black and White?" Dread washes over me. "What? What's he going to do?"

Ravin comes right up against me, her face so close to mine that I can see the individual hairs on her head. With barely contained anger, she says, "Stay out of this. It doesn't involve you." She shoves me aside and stalks away.

Cor is watching me. I turn to her. "Tell me. What's Mike going to do?"

She just shakes her head.

"It does too involve me, Cor. Tell me!"

Cor starts walking away. I can't believe she's doing this. "Cor!"

She turns, her face empty of all emotion. Flat. "After school, in the wood shop hall." She stands there, just looking at me. "If you really want to know."

It's gone beyond wanting to know. I have to know.

The clock creeps through the afternoon. Lex looks at me all through science, wounded and hopeful all in one. Mr. Inkster's riveting lecture today is on the life cycle of the fruit fly. Not much of a life, really. You hatch, you lay eggs, you die. I imagine fruit flies wearing sneakers and carrying backpacks in the nano-moment of their teens. Maybe, when life is so short, they don't waste any time tormenting one another. All for one, one for all, let's find some fruit.

I get down to the wood shop hall before Ravin and Cor. Just Mike is there — and his friends from auto shop. For a long and sickening moment I think Ravin and Cor have bailed and that I'm on my own. But they finally show up, along with a few people I haven't seen before. It strikes me that Nevkeet isn't here, and I can't remember when I last saw him. Ravin looks even paler than usual. Julian arrives after they do, and Cor gives him a little smile. I've never noticed before, but his eyelashes are pure white.

Ravin takes a position near the center. "This isn't going to work, Mike. Trashing cars is one thing, but actually attacking people?"

"It's just paint, Ravin. Picture it. The whole school dressed to the nines, all in black and white. We apply a judicious dose of red paint. It's like art. They are the canvas, we are the artist."

The guys laugh at this. Ravin shakes her head.

"So, REMBRANDT, how exactly will you apply the paint?"

Mike looks at his friends, a smirk on his face. "Super Splatters."

"Water guns?"

"Why not? Paint, water. Both are liquid."

"We make them custom," Julian says, "with gray PVC piping and a special valve so they don't clog. They look just like the real thing."

Cor eyes him with disbelief. "The real what?"

"Real guns."

Water. Paint. Blood. Red blood, spraying out of still, young bodies.

Ravin is moving the length of the group, fists white at her sides. "And how do you figure you'll get away with it?"

Mike shifts to face her. "Well, that's the beauty of it. No one will know who did it. Half the people at the dance will be wearing black. So will we. It'll be dark. We'll hide our faces. Only a few of us will have sprayers. The rest will be there as diversions." He pauses and something like a smile crosses his face. "It'll be like we all did it, but none of us did it."

Ravin stops in front of Mike, her face almost touching his. "But WE'LL know."

"So what's your point?" Mike shoulders past her and turns to the rest of us.

"That any one of us might get caught and end up taking the blame," Ravin states.

"There's always an element of risk." Mike looks from face to face. "Of course, if that person were to talk, then we'd all be caught. So we will make a pact. Every one of us."

His brown eyes meet every gaze, some excited, some afraid. Cor looks away and Mike turns her face toward his. "The need of the group is far greater than any individual need, wouldn't you agree, Cor?"

Cor shuffles, trying to pull back from him. Her chin is white under his thumb. "Inside this group, you are safe. Outside, you are alone. Everything you require is here. With us."

She nods.

Mike looks at me. In his face I see that list of names. How many more are on it? "And you, our young apprentice. We can count on your silence?"

I look over his shoulder at Ravin. She is pacing, back and forth along the same stretch of floor. Her eyes are on her shoes. She's sucked back into herself, and the rest of us aren't even here. Mike swings his face in front of mine. "Well, MARLENA? Are you in or out?"

The voice isn't mine. "I'm in."

Way too deep. I curl up on my bed and jam a pillow over my face. This doesn't feel right — Ravin knows it. So do I. It's gone beyond Nevkeet. It's all about Mike now. All about his hate list. I toss the pillow onto the floor and grab the phone.

"Nana? It's Marlie. No, we haven't heard anything. Yeah, I know. Listen, if Dad does call, would you tell him something for me? Tell him I want to go, too. I could meet up with him. No, I'm all right. I just need to be gone from here. No, I'm not in any trouble. I just need to be gone. Tell him, okay?"

Dad's been getting money from her for years. Sooner or later, he'll call. And then I can be gone.

CHAPTER TWENTY-FOUR

—〜〜—

"Chuck, it's Marlie." I can breathe easier here. It's like Chuck's workroom is a refuge, a place to pretend for awhile that life is normal.

"Hey," Chuck's voice grunts to me from behind a set of cabinets. "I'll. Be. Right. There."

I step over to the cabinets to see what he's doing. He's stretched out on the floor, his knees drawn up, his cheeks a deep pink. He's struggling to lift his head off the floor.

"What are you doing?"

Sweat glistens on Chuck's forehead. "Sit-ups. Isn't that rather obvious?"

"Not from you," I snort. "I've never seen you do any kind of exercise."

Chuck heaves himself onto an elbow and reaches for a water bottle. "Yeah, well, I'm a reformed man." He rolls over onto his hands and knees and slowly hoists himself off the floor. "I'm up to thirty, twice a day." He pats his soft mid-section. "Am I rippling yet?"

"Yeah, I hardly recognize you. So, you have a date or something?"

"Maybe." Chuck tosses me a bag of carrot sticks.

"Oh, no. Vegetables too? You should be careful you don't shock your system."

"I'm a well-oiled machine. So, did you bring your homework?"

"Math AND English."

"Hmm. Math is harder. Do it first."

"Not necessarily. Mrs. Pincott wants us to write a short story. She says to write about something we know. I thought I'd write something about an undertaker."

"Nah. It's overdone. Unless it's an undertaker with a twist."

I take a carrot stick from the bag and snap it with my teeth. "Are you really going on a date?"

Chuck eyes me. "Would that surprise you?"

"I'd say it's about time. Anyone I know?"

"Maybe."

"The undertaker cloaked himself in mystery. Only the shadows knew his real identity."

"Not bad. Do I get a bat cave?"

"Yeah. You could be Super-Romeo, a quiet undertaker by day, but by night, a love-crazed Titan. Your weakness will be fried chicken."

"Oh, don't talk about fried chicken." Chuck's belly rumbles loudly.

"And chocolate shakes."

"Stop already."

"Chuck, seriously, if this lady is worth your time, she should accept you just the way you are."

Chuck takes my hand and kisses it wetly. "Fair maiden, would that they all had your wisdom." He eyes my fingernails. "You're doing a good job on these."

I pull my hand from him and wipe it on my pants. "Kiss her like that and those sit-ups are wasted."

Chuck flips open a file folder of paperwork and chews the end of a blue pen. "Do your homework."

I pull my draft out of my pack and doodle around the holes. Mrs. Pincott said to write something I know. I'd been working on it for a few days and except for checking spelling, it was almost done.

"My story has girl characters. But I gave you a cameo appearance."

Chuck grunts.

"These aren't your princess types."

He looks up from his work. "No dragons?"

"That's right. And no knights." I scratch my name on the top of a clean page. "Dragons are just real-life problems morphed into something tangible, anyway."

"Like national debt?"

"Like ninth grade."

Chuck watches me over his stack of papers. "I hope these girl characters have good weapons."

I look over my draft, then write.

In the time of Starpath, great wars waged over the earth, and gentle people armed themselves with rocks and bows against the bloodthirsty soldiers that roamed the fields. No one knew why they were fighting, just that they had to fight, or else be killed.

Starpath learned to fight from her father, and when he was killed, she took up his weapons and led a gentle tribe of growers. Cornsilk, a healer's apprentice, was her best friend.

It was a dangerous time, and Starpath fought hard to defend the tribe from invaders, and also from those within, who sought to take her power for their own. One was more dangerous than any other. His name was Blaze.

Blaze would do anything to take over the tribe. One by one, with hollow promises and lies, he turned the tribe against Starpath. Only Cornsilk remained her loyal friend.

One day, when Cornsilk was in the meadows gathering healing herbs, Blaze and his followers besieged Starpath in her fortress, and set fire to it. She died without a cry.

Cornsilk took her friend's body, and wrapped it in cloth, like the ancients had taught her, sprinkling it with wild sage and her own tears. She covered the grave with rocks, a pile so high that it could be seen for miles around. Then she stood on the pile. And she screamed.

Crops bent in the fields and birds left their nests, never to return. The skies blackened and Cornsilk stood on top of the rocks, her screams like thunder. The people covered their ears and huddled together in fear. All except Blaze, that is. He just laughed.

The rocks started to shake, and the earth around the pile broke into wide cracks. Cornsilk's cry became a deep rumble, and the pile a mountain. People ran for their lives, but Blaze shook his fist, defying Cornsilk's anger. The mountain roared, and fire licked at its top. Boulders rolled like dust from the fiery volcano. Cornsilk cried again, and the mountain erupted, red rock rivers engulfing the tribe lands, the city, and Blaze himself.

Some say Cornsilk escaped the volcano, blown clear on its first hot breaths. Others say she jumped in to join her friend in death. No one knows, but Cornsilk was never seen again.

I give it to Chuck to read.

"Nice touch, sprinkling the body with sage. That would make me the ancient, I guess." He smiles, but his eyebrows are creased. He reads it again, the furrows on his forehead deepening.

"What, don't you like it?"

"No, it's good. It's really good. It's sad, that's all." He's reading the last paragraph again.

"It's just a story, Chuck. Don't get all choked up."

"Is it? It sounds, I don't know, desperate."

"Like it's something I know about?" I snap the pages out of his hand.

"Yes. Like it's something that's really happening."

Yeah. I should say, what's really happening, Chuck, is that the only friends I have scare the crap out of me. And what kind of loser does that make me? Maybe Keely and Loren were right about me. They just saw it before I did. And if you really knew who I was, then how long would you stick around? Yeah. I'll say that.

"Chuck, those sit-ups must have strained something in your brain." I stuff the story into my pack and pull out my math. "Either that or these carrots are good for seeing what's not there."

I ignore the concern on his face and toss him a carrot from the bag. "With some peanut butter, these would be almost edible."

CHAPTER TWENTY-FIVE

—ᴡᴡ—

The book Mrs. Grimshaw loaned me lies open on my pillow, the pages riffling of their own accord to a well-marked passage.

I wanted something to help me take my mind off Mike and the spray guns. All weekend, I wished that I hadn't gone down to the wood shop, that I hadn't heard Mike's manic plan. Then I could have gone on pretending that he's really not that dangerous. And now the dance is less than a week away.

I imagine Ms. Grimshaw reading this same passage. How old was she? What did she look like? Did she read it in bed, like I am, or in a chair with a proper light? Did she eat cookies while she read? I inspect the binding for crumbs. After all, Ms. Grimshaw wasn't always a librarian.

Some people, though, are born librarian-like. Elliott, for example, the way he sorts his stuff by category. But not his friend McLean.

I saw McLean in front of the house tonight, his coat undone, his hat twisted sideways, his nose running. He asked me if I thought it would snow again, because he wanted to go sledding with Elliott when he comes home. He must be really missing Elliott, if he's talking to me now. McLean has the same blue eyes that Keely has.

Then he asked me if I was going to get a nose ring. I pulled his hat down over his eyes and fake punched him in the stomach. McLean is okay.

I pick up the book and flip through, looking for a passage that I can decipher. I find one with no margin notes. Ms. Grimshaw must have missed this one. Or else didn't like it. It's entitled, ON FORGIVENESS.

I yawn. The occasional phrase grabs me, and I reread sentences to get the meaning, pausing at words that bring images to mind. What I think about most is Annie. I wonder if her parents ever forgave each other — or themselves. I wonder if they ever forgave their son.

I wonder if Chuck's brother, Sid, lies awake at night thinking about Annie, too.

I must have fallen asleep, because Mom's covered me up. She's sitting at the desk, Ms. Grimshaw's book open in front of her, rubbing one temple while she reads. Her face, still barely lined, holds the light from the bedside lamp like a gentle moon.

She sees me watching her and comes to sit on the side of my bed. "I'm going to borrow your book, okay?" She strokes the side of my head, like she used to do when I was little.

I nod, my eyes already closing. She snaps off the lamp and kisses me, lightly, on the top of the head.

"It looks like Chuck has given you a special book."

❧ ❧ ❧

It was a wicked dream, the kind that lures you in, all nice and pleasant, then BAM, you're wide awake with your heart pounding, thinking, "I'll never go to sleep again."

It was about Dad. He and Elliott and I were on a snowy mountainside, laughing as we got ready to sled down. Dad was in front on the sled, Elliott in the middle. I was standing behind the sled, just about to push us off. Then Dad's arms shot out beside the sled and he shoved it into motion. Elliott was laughing. Maybe he didn't know I wasn't on. I ran to catch them, but they were going too fast. Then the sled went faster, whistling between the trees. I called to them to slow down, but of course no sound came out. Elliott started to cry. They were rocketing toward the edge of the mountain. I screamed then, a silent dream scream. Dad turned around on the sled so he was facing Elliott. His face changed to sad. Then they vanished over the precipice.

The dream was still with me when I stood in the shower, that image of Dad's face, so hopeless, and it follows me to breakfast.

Mom is in her robe at the kitchen table, the newspaper open to the crossword, Ms. Grimshaw's book at her elbow by her coffee cup. The dream recedes as I think about what she said last night.

I motion to the book. "What makes you think that Chuck gave it to me?"

She picks up the book and opens it to the inscription. "I just assumed he did. This is his handwriting."

I take the book from her and study the inscription.

"Look," Mom says, pointing to the writing. "That is just the way Chuck makes his Cs, with the curly little flourish thing."

Ms. Grimshaw's enduring love is Chuck? My Chuck? No way.

"Ms. Grimshaw lent it to me," I say.

"Ms. Grimshaw?" Mom looks puzzled.

"The librarian," I explain.

"Oh. Then the little margin notes are hers too?"

"I guess. She must have made the notes before taking the Librarian's Oath — you know, 'Neither dog-ear nor deface.'"

"I read it last night. It was like it was speaking right to me. I couldn't put it down."

"You read the whole thing? Give me the condensed version, in case Ms. Grimshaw quizzes me." I put bread in the toaster and sit down at the table.

"Well, it's a book of essays. Some are funny. They're like lessons for living." Mom gets up to refill her coffee. "Did you read the one about forgiveness?"

"Actually I read it three times, trying to figure it out."

"That's where the quote comes from in the inscription." Mom leafs through to the passage and reads it aloud.

"'To mend your heart, only this: forgiveness, an antidote for the isolated life.'"

Maybe Ms. Grimshaw bought the book used.

My toast pops and I coat it thickly with cheese spread. Nevkeet once said cheese spread was only two ingredients away from green garbage bags.

Mom is stirring sugar into her coffee, the spoon clinking the sides of the cup like a bell. "I've been angry at your father for so long it's become who I am."

I think of the picture of her in the slinky dress and pointed shoes, and it makes me wonder who my mother was, before she met my dad. The dream comes back to me — his face before they vanish.

"Are you saying you can forgive Dad?"

Mom sighs and brings her eyes up to mine. "I want to try."

"You hung in with Dad for a long time. He needs to grow up." I could tell her my dream, but it would send her into a fit of worry. My father needs to bring Elliott home so we can all get on with our lives!

She sips her coffee then sets it down and sighs again. "Do you think you can ever forgive me?"

I swallow a mouthful of toast, hard. "For making me wear that dress to Cousin Myron's wedding?"

Mom reaches over and closes her hand over mine. "I do love him, even now, with what he's done. There's a part of me he owns. But I need to grow up too." She squeezes my hand. "And there's so much of your dad in you."

❖ ❖ ❖

How hard can it be, I wonder as I walk to the library at lunch. I'll just ask her. "Ms. Grimshaw," I'll say, "did you ever swap spit with Chuck Mann?"

Or, I could just find out if her first name is Clarice. She's out of the library when I get there. Her gym bag is sitting by the coat rack. She'll have her name in the bag. Probably in permanent ink, on a laminated label.

The quiet guy from grade ten is back, a stack of books

in front of him. No one else is in the library. I squat down beside the bag.

The zipper sounds like a freight train. I glance up at Quiet Guy. His head is still bent to his work.

Carefully, so as not to disturb anything, I look inside the bag. A soft green towel is folded on top, then slithery shorts and tank top, then a serious pair of workout shoes. I can't see a tag. Along one side of the bag is a paisley fabric pouch, the kind you put toiletries in. I run my hand down the inside of the bag, feeling for a label. My hand closes on something cold, and I pull it partway out to see what it is.

It is a bag of carrot sticks.

I must have sat there, holding that bag of carrots, absolutely stunned, because the sound of Ms. Grimshaw's voice knocks me on my butt.

"And just what do you think you're doing?" Ms. Grimshaw snatches the carrots out of my hand, stuffs them into the gym bag, and yanks the zipper closed.

"Mrs. Birk said it was probably you who had used my computer and left it on." She's got her laser-glare eyes set to liquefy. "But I said, no, that Marlie Peters is a hard-working volunteer. Not a snoop. Or a thief."

"This isn't what it looks like." It sounds lame, even to me.

"Oh, save it," she snaps. "I could have helped you. This isn't an easy school sometimes." She drops into her chair, her arms crossed, her black hair wild at the temples. "But you don't want any help, do you? You can manage just fine all on your own. You maybe even like this path of self-destruction."

She's thinking about something more serious than thieving carrot sticks. The most bizarre feeling comes over me, like some out-of-body experience where I'm watching myself, sitting on the floor, and Ms. Grimshaw knows everything. Mike, my dad — she knows everything about me. The image-me blurs, like the secrets are my skeleton and without them I'm a glutinous blob. I blink and take a deep breath. "Ms. Grimshaw, do you play chess?"

Her eyes narrow, and she sniffs at my words like a dog at something dead. "How is that relevant?"

"It's not." I get up off the floor. The steam around her seems to be dissipating. "I'm just curious."

"Well, yes, I do play chess. Although I haven't played for a long time."

"Are you any good?"

Ms. Grimshaw lets out an exasperated sigh. "Why?"

I bow my head. "I'm sorry I got into your bag."

Ms. Grimshaw opens her mouth to say something, then clamps it closed.

"Ms. Grimshaw, would you play chess with me sometime? I'm just learning and could use some, uh, guidance." Ms. Grimshaw uncrosses her arms. The fire in her eyes subsides. Am I good or what?

"Well, yes, I suppose we could do something like that."

"Thanks. That would be great. I'll just start on the shelving, then." I turn to leave her office. "Oh, and I'll bring your book back tomorrow. It's got some great stuff in it. Like on forgiveness."

"Yes," she sniffs. "I'm glad it's been helpful."

I hope she reads *that* chapter.

"Marlie."

I turn to her voice.

"I'll hold you to it. The chess, I mean."

"Yes. I'll look forward to it." And I will. Chuck and Ms. Grimshaw. Isn't that a thought.

I'm taking an armful of books to the 300s when I notice Quiet Guy in happy conversation with someone. The kid's back is to me, but I recognize the voice.

"Nevkeet! I haven't seen you for a while!"

His face takes on the most appalling shade of olive green, and he stands back from the table, his eyes darting around as if he's looking for someone.

"Hi, Marlie. Nice to see you. I was just leaving."

Quiet Guy is looking from Nevkeet to me, puzzled.

"Well, then I'll walk you out." I set the books down on the table.

His skin takes on a deeper green.

He goes straight for the door and I have to practically run to keep up.

"Nevkeet, what is the matter with you?"

At first I don't think he's going to answer me. He's already out in the hall when he finally turns to me.

"They broke my violin that day." Sweat is beading on his upper lip. "But that's all. Mike did the rest. For effect, he said." Nevkeet holds his elbows close to his chest. "He said he was just going to rough up my clothing."

"Nevkeet . . ."

"He liked it, hurting me. When I started to cry, he hit me more."

I shake my head, not because I don't believe him, but because I don't want to.

"I thought I could trust him. I thought I was his friend."

There are no friends. "I'm not his friend, Nevkeet."

He shrugs, impatient. "So why are you still with him?"

"I'm not. I mean, some of my friends are, that's all."

"Some friends."

I open my mouth to protest, but he cuts me off. "With a guy like Mike, you're with him or you aren't. Not that either position guarantees he won't stick you." He looks both ways in the corridor. "Because if he wants to, he will. Just because he can."

Quiet Guy comes out of the library and it's like Nevkeet doesn't know me anymore. Without another word, not even a parting glance, Nevkeet joins him and walks away.

CHAPTER TWENTY-SIX

—◦◦◦—

Mike and Julian are waiting with Ravin after school. For a heart-stopping moment I'm afraid that somehow, Mike has found out that Nevkeet spoke to me. But when I come up to them, he nods to me. "We're going to the mall. Come with us." If I want to get Ravin alone to tell her about Nevkeet, then I have to go along.

"Is Cor coming?" I say to Julian.

"No," he blurts. Then he blinks about a hundred times and says, "I mean, we didn't ask her. Because she's studying." He doesn't look at me when he says this.

Not a bad thought, studying. If you can forget that in four days your friends are going to pull paint guns on the school dance. And we'll be lucky if that's all Mike has in mind.

Mike and Ravin walk ahead of us, discussing a movie that was on last night. Julian is silent. Finally, I ask him, "Why do they have to look like the real thing?"

He turns to me, puzzled.

"I mean the paint sprayers. Why do they have to look like guns?"

One side of his mouth lifts up and he says, like I should know this, "Because all sprayers look like guns."

Not all sprayers are the colorless gray of real metal.

"So they'll look like handguns, like Ravin's mom's?"

"That little bitty thing?" He shakes his head. "I don't think so."

There's a perfume smell at the mall. Not the clouds that the white-coated ladies spray at the fancy cosmetic counters. Just a smell. Like they pipe it in through the vents or something. I used to like it, when it meant trying on clothes with Keely. Now it makes my eyes hurt.

In the center courtyard, an underfed Santa slumps on his throne, while an elf assistant with a short skirt and clumpy mascara leans on a candy-striped pole, chewing gum. There's not a kid in sight. I used to try to protect Elliott from this seasonal shabbiness, but then last year, as he wrote his letter to Santa, he told me, "I know he's not real. But I still like the thought." His letter asked for the usual ream of stuff, then in big letters, "and please help my dad to be happy."

At the DeeJay Music store, Julian pauses at the window.

"Ravin, do you want to see if the new *Badblood* CD is in?"

"It won't be. I checked a couple of days ago."

The blink is back. "We're right here. Let's see what else has come in."

She shrugs and we start to go in. A sign on the door says "ONLY THREE STUDENTS IN STORE AT ONE TIME."

"Marlie, you wait with Mike out here," Julian says,

pointing to a bench outside the store.

"No," I say quickly. "That's okay. I'll go with you guys."

Julian glances at Mike.

Mike smiles a little and says, "Suit yourself."

The store clerk, a guy around twenty with Buddy Holly glasses and bad skin, looks up as we come in. "Check your bags." He gestures to Julian's and my backpacks. I drop mine beside Julian's in a bin at the door.

"This too?" Ravin shows him her shoulder bag. She never carries a pack. I don't think she ever brings books home. "It's a purse."

The store clerk shrugs and returns to a textbook open in front of him.

Ravin and Julian move through the aisles, flipping racks of CDs and saying nothing. I wander over to the counter to read a poster of upcoming concerts.

At the counter is a stack of some obscure elevator music. It's the kind of thing Ms. Grimshaw might buy. The cover shows a lake at sunset. "Clearance. $3.99."

Ravin joins me at the counter. "Good luck selling them at that price," she says, indicating with her head the sunset special. "Come on. Let's go." She starts for the door.

Suddenly Julian shoves between us, knocking me against the counter. A can of Coke teeters on the edge of the clerk's textbook.

"Hey!" The clerk glares at me. He obviously thinks I'm a half-wit.

"Sorry," I say.

I pass the glare on to Julian. But then I wish I hadn't. Because I see Julian sliding one of the cheap CDs into Ravin's bag. And she's headed for the door. My mouth drops open and maybe I could stop her, except my feet are stuck and my brain's frozen, and anyway, she moves too fast.

The sensor at the door goes off like a siren. The store clerk jumps, jamming the glasses up on his nose and bolting around the side of the counter.

Ravin is standing in the doorway, a stunned look on her face. She looks at me, then at Julian, and I know in that moment that she has no idea what Julian did.

A uniformed security guard with a big gut is huffing into the store. He turns off the alarm, and the silence rings louder in my ears. "I'll check your bag, miss."

Without a word, Ravin holds open her bag. The stolen CD is lying right on top. Bright spots of color rise on Ravin's cheeks, and she looks at Julian with narrowed eyes.

The security guard pushes Julian and me toward the door. "You two get out of here. We need to have a word with your little friend."

I look back at Ravin. She's standing with her arms crossed, her eyes up to the ceiling. She won't look at me.

Julian's face is bright red. He grabs his pack and leaves. I take mine, too, but I'm afraid to go through the sensor. I don't think he's planted anything on me, but the siren terrifies me. The security guard gives me a shove. "Out of here." The siren doesn't go off. "Right out of here." He jerks his thumb at the mall exit.

Ravin's back is to me now. The store clerk is on the phone to someone. Maybe the police. The security guard turns back into the store. His blue-shirted bulk blocks Ravin completely.

Julian bursts for the mall exit. I stumble from the store, stopping in front of Mike who is smiling smugly. He puts his hand on my elbow, turning me toward the street exit. It's like I don't have knees anymore. My hands drop to my sides. I don't have any strength. Not even to breathe. He leads me out of the mall. Julian is on the sidewalk, taking big breaths.

"That wasn't so hard, was it?" Mike's voice is oily. Pleased. It snaps me back.

I pull my arm away from him and shout at Julian, "Why? Why did you do that?"

His cheeks clench and unclench. "I've got to go." He turns quickly and strides away.

Mike watches him, a small smile on his lips. Then he says, quietly, "Because I told him to." He turns to me, the smug look on his face making me want to slap him. "That sure put Ravin in her place. And I guess I found out what side you're on, too." His mouth widens to a leer. "Mine."

I pull a breath in, so angry I can't form words.

He laughs, then calls to Julian. "Wait up."

Julian stops, but doesn't turn around. Mike jogs up to him, and they leave me there on the sidewalk. I don't think I've ever been more alone.

✤ ✤ ✤

The board fence in the walkway by Ravin's house is hard against my back. She's a long time coming home.

Her mother's white minivan lurches around the corner at the end of the street and rolls to a stop on the driveway. I duck down, so her mother won't see me.

Ravin's mother gets out with a fat black briefcase. Her skirt creases like a fan where she's been sitting. She's stabbing at her eyes with a tissue.

"I used to be able to count on you. Now you are one unhappy surprise after another." She's mad, but the way she says it, I know she's hurting more.

Ravin is walking behind her mother, her head lowered. Black streaks run down both her cheeks.

"I'm sorry, okay? I don't know why I did it, okay? It'll never happen again, okay?"

"Just get up to your room. We'll talk about this when your father gets home."

"Like next week." Ravin says it quietly, but her mom spins on her heels.

"I've just about had it with you and your attitude." She turns to the house and unlocks the door. "You don't know how good you've got it."

The front door clicks closed, and I wait for the light to come on in Ravin's window.

There's no point ringing the bell. Mrs. Hughes isn't going to let me in. But I have to see Ravin. With my heart pounding in my ribs, I slowly open the front door and step in.

I can hear water running in the kitchen. As quietly as I can, I climb the stairs to Ravin's room.

Ravin hardly looks at me when I open her door. She is drawn up on her bed, her chin on her knees. The rim of red in her eyes makes mine want to water.

"So," she says, "we're initiated."

"Why didn't you say something? Mike made him do it, you know."

With a sneer she says, "And Julian always does what

he's told."

"Why did you let him get away with it?"

Ravin pushes her fingers through her hair. "It's not really about Julian, is it? It's about Mike. Mike might think I let him get away with it. He might think it means something. But it doesn't."

She sits back against the wall and crosses her arms. Her eyes are cold.

"And I didn't hear you saying anything."

I feel my cheeks redden. I could lie, say I didn't see him do it, or that I tried to warn her and she was at the door before I could, but it won't change what happened, or what's happening.

"Ravin, I'm sorry."

"You don't need to be sorry. If it had been you, I probably wouldn't have said anything, either."

It's not meant to make me feel better.

"Can't Julian see that Mike is using him?" I say.

"Oh, probably." Ravin shrugs. "Some people like dangerous friends. It makes them feel powerful."

I tell her about Nevkeet.

Ravin shakes her head. "Mike, he was a mistake." She rolls off the bed and stands at the window. "Nevkeet told me and Cor, right after it happened."

"You knew?" I can't keep the disgust out of my voice.

She chews at the skin around her thumb. "It would have frightened you if I'd told you. And the others, too."

No, really? Wouldn't want everyone bailing on you, would you?

Nice of Cor to tell me.

The sky has darkened to evening. Ravin's back is to me,

and she's talking to me, or her reflection in the window, I can't tell which. "The whole thing has gone bad. We used to be together for moral support or just not to be alone. But so long as we're together, then Mike is my problem. And I can handle Mike."

She's just been caught shoplifting. At what cost will she handle Mike? And who's going to pay?

"I wrote a story for English about a guy who has too much power. Cor read it and said it made her think of Mike."

"You wrote about us?" Ravin asks coldly.

"No, not about us. The guy's name was Blaze—"

She interrupts me. "That sounds like the name of a horse. Maybe you wrote a horse story." There's clearly a threat in her voice. "Everybody loves horse stories, Marlie."

The story is due tomorrow. There is no way I can rewrite it. "You'd think I wrote it about a girl charged with shoplifting."

She turns from the window then. "I won't be charged, considering my dad is a member."

My mouth must be gaping open.

"Yeah. Cop's daughter goes bad. Now there's a story."

Cooking smells are coming up the stairs. Mom will be getting squirrelly that I'm not home yet.

"I've got to go."

Ravin waves me off. "I'll go down first." She doesn't say goodbye. I stand at her bedroom door for a while, thinking she'll give me a signal, an all-clear or something. She doesn't. I creep down the stairs and out into the dark.

CHAPTER TWENTY-SEVEN

~~~

I am truly desperate if I'm going to see Mrs. Birk. But all last night I saw Mike's smirk, and his spray guns, and Julian saying, "That little bitty thing?" Then I got thinking about the car fire. And the smoke bomb. And it occurred to me: I just had to get Mike suspended. Then we'd all be off the hook for the dance.

The chairs outside Mrs. Birk's office are curved, made of wood, with arms on them that circle around like real arms. Someone has scratched their initials with blue pen. "I.M." I try to think of anyone with the initial "I." I can't even think of a name that begins with "I."

Mrs. Orthney is clattering away on her keyboard. She had looked up when I came in, her eyes widening a bit as she remembered the last time I was there and the mess in Mrs. Birk's office.

"I need to see Mrs. Birk. It's important."

She gave me a look that said, "yeah, right," and told me to sit. Now I'm watching her brown dress where it bunches under her chair and thinking that if those shoes were any more sensible, they'd be men's.

Mr. Bates, the guidance counselor, comes out of the principal's office. If a human being could be twisted like a rag doll, that would be Mr. Bates. He stands outside the door and blinks, like he's trying to remember where he is. He sees me.

"Oh, good morning Marlie." He comes over. He's wearing a yellow turtleneck, and it almost matches his pallor. "Any news about Elliott?"

"No. Not yet."

"I'm sorry to hear that. How are you keeping?" His eyes are a little clearer now. He's trying hard.

"I'm okay. How are you?"

He looks over his shoulder at Mrs. Birk's office. "I've had better days. Are you next?"

I smile at him. "Yeah. Any advice?"

He leans his head toward mine. "She's taking no prisoners."

Mrs. Orthney rolls back from her desk. "Marlena? Mrs. Birk will see you now." She stands at the principal's door like a sentry, my manila file in her hand.

Mr. Bates gives me a thumbs-up. I wonder what he was trying to extract from Mrs. Birk. More pop machines, maybe. Mrs. Orthney waves me into the office.

Mrs. Birk is writing on a lined yellow pad when I come in. I stand at her desk, watching her. I have a clear view of her razor-straight part. She looks up, finally, and sees me. She pushes back from her desk a little, trying not to let me see her do it.

"Sit down, Marlena, please."

"It's Marlie."

"Oh yes. Marlie." She says it like its French or something. Mar Lay. "How can I help you today?" Translation: How can I get you out of my office.

"I know who set the smoke bomb."

Mrs. Birk puts down her pen. Her eyes in her fancy glasses pierce mine. "Who?"

"Mike Allard."

A whole palette of looks crosses Mrs. Birk's face. First one eyebrow comes up. Then both eyebrows scrunch together. Then both go up and she sits back in her chair.

"Mike Allard. Well, that's interesting. How do you happen to know this?"

"I heard it. From one of his friends."

"And you're not one of his friends?"

"Well, not really. I mean . . ."

"What is this friend's name?"

I stumble a bit on that. "I don't know. Or I'm not sure."

"So you heard something from someone you don't know about Mike, who is not your friend." Mrs. Birk picks up her pen and taps it on the desk. She leans forward and flips open a slim leather daily planner. She turns to a page with many yellow sticky notes.

"This is the day in question." She looks down her nose at the planner. "The occurrence was just before the afternoon bell. 12:53 to be exact. And this is interesting." She turns the planner so I can see it. Her pen is pointing to the entry at 12 noon. "Detention, Mike Allard."

I look up from the planner. Mrs. Birk is half-smiling. "Our friend Mike was here. With me. He couldn't have set a bomb. You, or should I say your friend, must be mistaken."

"But . . ."

"That will do, Marlena. Please return to class."

I get up to leave. I can feel Mrs. Birk staring into my back.

"And, Marlena." I turn back to her. "Ms. Grimshaw told me about the little incident with her things."

I could die now. Right here, in a messy liquid pile. Right on her carpet.

"You must be careful not to get a reputation for being a troublemaker. It can follow you all through school."

With sudden clarity I see those initials, I.M., placed with a surname, as in, I.M. Scrude.

I nod, because I can't think of anything to say, but I want to get out of there.

"Thank you, Marlena. Come and see me anytime."

☆ ☆ ☆

I've tiptoed around the school all morning trying to avoid Mike. When I told Ravin what I'd done, she said it was a stupid move, and that I should have talked to her first.

She said the shoplifting thing was just a practical joke.

Two more days until the dance. She said we'd pull the dance stunt, then she'd dissolve the group. She still thinks she can handle Mike. She said it was just paint.

At lunch who should come in to the library, carrying a bright green slushy for me from the corner store, but Mike. And Ravin, too, right on his heels. Her eyes look hollow and scared. Mike looks like life couldn't be better.

"I've promoted you." He hands me the slushy. "For the dance." He smiles.

I look at Ravin, but she avoids my eyes.

"You now have the honor of wearing this." He tosses a plastic bag on the desk. "Open it. I want to see how you look."

It's a black knit hat, the kind that folds down over your face. The kind criminals wear.

"Put it on."

Ravin is looking anywhere but in my direction.

He follows my eyes. "She got one too. It looks really good." Mike's lips are wet and his eyes are too bright.

I swallow. "What if I don't want to wear it?"

He laughs. "You've given up that choice."

I must look as green as the slushy. He laughs again. "I did do it, you know. The smoke bomb. Right from Fiona's office. She was standing at the photocopier yapping to someone. It was a perfect alibi. She didn't even notice. I have one in my garage I could set here tomorrow and she still wouldn't suspect me. She had a good laugh this morning telling me that some ninth-grade girl had fingered me for it."

Ravin plasters an 'I told you so' look on her face.

"Put it on." He's not laughing anymore.

I pull the cap over my head. It's hot and the fibers make my nose itch. In a strange way, I feel better with my face covered, like an ostrich that puts its head in the sand. I leave the eyeholes on top of my head, and pull tufts of hair through. I can still see through the holes in the knit. Ravin is almost smiling. Mike isn't.

"Are you looking for the tag?" Mike says with a sneer. "Do you need the instructions?"

"No. I like it this way." I bump against the desk, because I can't see that well. I giggle nervously. "I'm going to wear it this afternoon. I'll be able to walk down the hall without Loren seeing me."

"Take it off." Ravin sounds serious.

The library is quiet. Weird quiet. I yank off the hat.

Mike and Ravin are gone. Mr. Bates is in the doorway. He looks pale.

Slowly, like he's thinking about each step, he moves toward me. He reaches out his hand.

"Give it to me."

I hand him the hat. He takes it, all the time looking at me, his eyes fixed like probes.

"The last time I saw one of these, there was a hole the size of a grapefruit blown out the back."

He looks at the balaclava, laying it out on the desk, smoothing it with his hands.

"The kid who had it was fifteen." His hands move like the hat is a face. "They thought he had a gun."

He looks at me. "They didn't tell him they were going to steal anything. He was just out with his friends."

Folding the hat neatly into a bundle, Mr. Bates presses it in my hand. I'm trying hard to keep my face expressionless. Mike could be just around the door. I wonder what he'd do if he heard me telling everything to Mr. Bates. Mr. Bates would believe me, I know he would. Maybe he could actually do something about Mike, if he could go over Mrs. Birk, that is. Then I'd only have to live in perpetual fear that Mike, or one of his friends, would play some 'practical joke' on me.

If anything happened to me, Mom would be over the edge in a flash. I take the hat from Mr. Bates.

He looks at the slushy, now melted into green syrup.

"Ever notice what floats in those after they melt?" He lifts the cup and tilts it so I can see. "Bits of crud from the machine, from people's hands, who knows what."

Mr. Bates is right. It looks like green lake water, silted with sludge. "You just don't notice all of it there when the stuff is frozen. You can't see it." He tosses it into the garbage.

He moves toward the door, then stops, and turns. He's looking at the floor.

"You know," he says, "in the Middle Ages, it wasn't just the executioners that covered their faces." When he looks at me, his eyes have a hardness I've never seen before. "The victims were hooded, too."

CHAPTER TWENTY-EIGHT

After school I bolt out, barely stopping at my locker to grab my coat. The afternoon air is brittle, and burns in my throat as I walk, fast, from the school. I don't want to see Mike again today. I don't want to see anyone except Chuck.

As I'm just about to open Chuck's door, Sid bursts out, pushing a casket on a trolley. I have to jump backward so that I don't get run over.

"Sorry," he says, clearly distracted. He swings the trolley around in the hall and barrels toward the service elevator. He jabs the button on the elevator panel, then pulls the white handkerchief from his suit pocket and mops his forehead. The doors slide open and he shoves the trolley into the elevator, disappearing with it.

I imagine Sid wearing the balaclava. Maybe he'd wear it back to front, so that he wouldn't have to see. Poor Annie. I open the door to Chuck's workroom and step in.

Chuck is a flurry of white lab coat and wrinkled Dockers. He's yanking rollers out of one gray head and winding them into another.

"Grab a lab coat, Marlie. It's flu season, and they're stacked up three deep in the cold room."

I put on a coat from the peg on the door and snap on latex gloves. I start on a woman's nails. Her hand feels heavy in mine. Heavy and cool. "What color does she want?"

"Check her chart. I think she's just a wax buff."

I flip open a file on the end of the woman's table. Her name is Ivy. In her picture, grown children, all smiling, surround her. They'll miss her. I take the suede nail buffer and run it over Ivy's nails until they gleam. She has nice nails. It feels good to be doing something nice for her, kind of like having a friend. Okay, a dead friend, but at least the relationship is all out in the open — dead friends don't betray. Besides, the work takes my mind off Mike.

"I'll start on her makeup."

Chuck releases a desperate sigh. "Be careful. Don't get any in her hair."

"I know that." I tie a cotton headband on her forehead to lift the curls out of the way.

"And don't use too much color. She's very fair."

"Gee, Chuck, I was thinking of stripes."

"Ah, I'm sorry. It's just been crazy in here."

"Maybe you're not eating enough." I look at Chuck's lab coat. It does seem to lie a little flatter in front.

"No. I ate lunch. A bagel, dry, with non-fat milk and a banana."

"Oh, well, yeah, that'll keep you going. I'll finish with Ivy then I'll get you some real food."

Ivy's skin is papery thin and so white that it is almost

blue. I pick a blusher the color of white roses and dust it over her cheekbones. For her lips, I find the palest pink, and brush it carefully into the fine lines and creases.

"Did you blend down her neck?"

"Yes, Chuck."

"Because there's nothing worse than a high water mark."

"I did!"

"Okay, okay." He comes over and gives Ivy a quick inspection. "You did good." The admiration in his voice makes me blush. He wheels Ivy back to the cold room. I start on the next table.

"Do you ever run into Clarice? Like at the vegetable store or anything?"

Chuck shoots me a look. "Why are you so interested?"

"No reason. I just thought you might see her. At the LIBRARY, or something."

"No. Not at the LIBRARY. Or anywhere. She wouldn't recognize me, anyway, and I have no idea of what she looks like now."

"So she's not your date?"

"Oh!" Chuck laughs. "No. Your mother is, actually."

"MOM!"

"Well, it's not really a date. We're going to your dance. As chaperones."

Chaperones. Dance. "You can't!"

He's grinning at me. "What, I can't go out with your mother?"

"No! I mean, yes. But not to the dance." I can't think of anything I'd like better than Chuck and Mom being together. But not at the Black and White. Not anywhere near Mike. "Couldn't you go to a movie like normal people?"

"Well, like I said, it's not really a date. Mr. Bates called your mom, to see if she'd work the dance. And your mom asked me if I'd go with her."

"Mr. Bates called Mom? Why Mom? There are only about three thousand other parents he could have asked. Did he ask everyone's mother to be a chaperone?" And if you don't take her to the dance, does that mean there's no date?

Chuck is finishing the next woman's hair with a curling iron. His back is to me. "I think he's concerned about you, Marlie. He's worried about this dance."

"And having my mother there is going to fix everything? I don't think so."

Chuck doesn't say anything.

"I mean, I think it's great you and Mom are going together. I really do. I thought with the sit-ups and carrots it was someone else."

"Like Clarice?"

"I'm really glad it's Mom." She needs you, Chuck. I need you.

"It's not a date."

"Yeah, yeah. You know, you've covered for Dad for too long. Even before Mom and Dad split up. Remember that father-daughter cookout in Brownies we did? And when you took me for ice cream after I flunked swimming lessons?"

"I'd do that for you anyway, Marlie."

"Well, maybe it's time you started thinking about what's

good for you. You'd like this to be a date, wouldn't you?"

Chuck sighs. The curling iron hisses a bit in the still-damp hair. "I'm nuts about your mother. I always have been."

"Well, you better get on it. Mom doesn't want to be alone, either. Maybe Mr. Bates is harboring indecent thoughts about her. That's why he wants her to come to the dance. Which, by the way, you two cannot go to."

"I think Mr. Bates's intentions are honorable. And why can't we go?"

I struggle for a bit. I wish I could talk to him, but what would I say? That it's going to get ugly? Because people are going to get sprayed with red paint? Because maybe Mike has something else in mind, and maybe some people are going to get hurt? And most of all, that I hate myself for knowing this, for letting it get this far.

"Because I'm not going."

"Since when?"

"Since right now."

Chuck is thinking about what to say. I can always tell when he's thinking, by the way his jaw flexes.

"What are you really afraid of?"

"I'm not afraid. I just changed my mind about going."

"What do you think is going to happen at that dance?"

"Why do you think I think something is going to happen?"

Chuck turns to me, slowly, the curling iron like a sword in his hand. "Because Mr. Bates is afraid something is going to happen. And when you talk about the dance, I hear that fear in your voice."

"So that's why you're going? So you can be Sir Charles, knight in shining armor?"

"Maybe. Is that so bad?"

"No. I wish I could be a knight too. We could fight the forces of evil together."

"Okay, but this time I get a bat cave."

"I love you, Chuck. You know?"

"I love you, too. And, yes, I know."

❖ ❖ ❖

"I've committed to being a chaperone. I'm not about to back out now!" Mom lobs a carton of milk back into the fridge and slams the door.

Our supper dishes are stacked beside the sink, crusting up nicely, no doubt.

"Why are you being so stubborn?" she says.

I block her path to the sink. "Stubborn? Me? You're the one who won't listen to reason. This is my school, Mom, not yours, and it's my dance. I don't want you there."

"Mr. Bates is short of parents. I couldn't possibly back out now, just two nights before the dance. You haven't given me any good reasons why I shouldn't be there, just that you don't want me there — I'm chaperoning that dance."

"Then I'm not going."

"Fine. I'll be there, with or without you."

I pull out a phrase I've heard before. "You're not respecting my feelings."

That makes her pause. With an exasperated sigh, she says, "I'm sorry. I should have talked to you before I promised Mr. Bates. And I will next time. But I'm going to the Black and White, and so is Chuck, because it's the right thing to do. You're just going to have to live with it." She steps around me and starts water running into the sink.

I'd like to throw those dirty dishes against the wall. I'd like to throw every dish we own against the wall. I'd like to scream, "Can't you see that I'm afraid for you?" I pace back and forth behind her, chewing on my lip. Then I say, "What if Elliott shows up on the doorstep, all alone at night, and there's no one here to let him in?"

Her hands stop moving in the sink, and her shoulders become very still. Then her head droops and I can see that she's crying. I watch her for a minute, wanting to say something, like I'm sorry. I'm sorry for this whole mess. Then I leave her there, alone, sobbing in the dishwater.

CHAPTER TWENTY-NINE

~~~~

As I'm gathering my books out of my locker before morning classes, I'm suddenly aware that someone is standing right behind me. I spin and come face to face with the huge bulk of Lex. His eyes widen, and sweat breaks out in shiny beads on his forehead.

"Hey, Marlie. Are you going to the dance tomorrow night?"

I wonder if I look as stunned as I feel.

"The Black and White," he says. "You know about it, right?"

Oh, Lex. I wish I didn't. "Uh, yeah, I don't know. I mean, I've heard it's a real show, with limos and tuxedos . . ."

"You don't have to dress really fancy, not if you don't want to."

"And I'm not much of a dancer."

"Me neither. Not that anyone would dance with me. But I like to listen to the music."

I turn and close my locker. To my back, he says, "We could go together."

"No." It comes out too loud, too sharp. I turn around.

"This dance isn't going to be any fun."

His cheeks get pink, and he says, "I wasn't asking you out or anything. I already have my ticket. I was just wondering if you were going."

"I'm sorry, Lex."

He shuffles away from me. "No. Don't be sorry. You're probably right. It'll probably be just a bunch of overdressed losers there." His face is now radiating pink.

Cor appears beside me. She smiles at Lex. "Am I interrupting?"

He looks at her and the color blanches from his face. His mouth gapes and closes like a fish. When he speaks, he actually stutters.

"I w-was just g-going."

I wish I could reach out and grab him, stop him from leaving. "I'm so sorry." But he doesn't hear me. He's already lost in the hallway crowd.

"So," Cor says. "What did Mrs. Pincott think of your Starpath story?"

I'm watching Lex's head bobbing above the crowd. "Not much. I didn't hand it in." I turn to her. "Where have you been? I haven't seen you all week."

Cor waves off my question. "Had the flu." She plants her hands on her hips. "Why didn't you hand in the story?"

I shrug. "Ravin thought it was too close to reality. I didn't have time to write anything else, so I just took the 'F.'"

Cor shakes her head. "Well, that was brilliant."

"I'll make it up. Stop sounding like somebody's mother."

"It'll lower your entire term average."

"Whatever."

She just looks at me. "You shouldn't let people push you around."

✧ ✧ ✧

"I'm not going to the dance." I yank a piece of mending tape over the spine of an ancient encyclopedia as Ravin eyes me from under a black ball cap.

She's just told Cor about the shoplifting. Cor is standing at the circulation desk, her arms crossed. Her lips are very tight.

"What Mike made Julian do just reinforces why we have to be there," Ravin says. "Mike is spinning wild. He has to be controlled. Besides, I'm not giving up on everyone else."

"There is no 'everyone else!'" I say. "Not for you. Not anymore. It's just Mike and his friends. And Julian. And us."

Ravin pulls off her cap. The part in her hair looks like it's an inch wide because of the way the lighter hair is growing in. It looks like a highway through a grain field, only in reverse. She scratches her head, then crams the hat back on.

"It's the principle of the thing," she says.

"What did that ever change? Did the skating stunt change anything? No! It just got you out of Lindsay's way. The stupid dance shouldn't even happen. We should leave Mr. Bates an anonymous note."

"Oh that would be good," Ravin says, rolling her eyes. "Like he wouldn't know who sent it? Why did he come to the library? Why did he call your mother?"

"He called mine too," Cor says, her voice small.

Ravin jabs her finger at me, "See? Oh yeah. Telling Bates would be really good. He wouldn't be in with Fiona longer than three minutes before she had everything from him, including how it is that we know so much. Me and Mike. Yeah. My dad would be thrilled to find out he compromised his position on the force for me, just so I could cover for a scumbag juvie."

"You covered for Julian."

"Mike, Julian, it's the same thing. Cor doesn't need any more trouble. Ms. Grimshaw already has you pegged as a petty thief. How much more grief do you want?"

"Mike is using us. We don't know what he's really planning for the dance. What if people get hurt. How long are we going to cover for him?"

Cor's voice is hardly above a whisper. "How will people get hurt?"

"I don't know," I say. "You know him better than anyone. You tell us."

Cor wraps herself in her arms. "Maybe he's harmless."

"Nevkeet doesn't think so," I say. "Mike was kind enough to rearrange his face. For the PRINCIPLE of the thing."

Cor's hair today is fire-engine red. Her face goes pure white and she slumps back against the desk.

Yeah, thanks for telling me.

Ravin sidles in at Cor's side. "Cor's right," she says. "Mike may be wild, but he's nothing I can't handle."

I say to her, "So you have a plan?"

"I'll watch him."

"That's it? You'll watch him?"

She shakes her head at me. "Why can't you trust me?"

"So you're both going to go?" I ask in disbelief.

Cor looks blankly out the window. Ravin chews on her thumbnail.

I let the encyclopedia thump onto the table. "Well, I guess I don't plan on surviving this alone." Mom is going to the dance, and Chuck, Lex, these two — and then there's Elliott. I can hardly bring his face to mind anymore. I wonder if Dad has a picture of Mom and me, so Elliott can look at it. So he can remember.

For better or worse, I won't be left behind again.

CHAPTER THIRTY

~~~

Maybe Chuck goes for the sword and shield stuff, but if there's one thing I've learned about fighting dragons, it's that you need fire power.

"What do you think of this? Is it too fancy?" Mom is holding up her little black dress, the one with the satin bow at the back.

"Not if you're planning on Chuck wearing a tux. And if you are, get over it."

Mom and I have reached an uneasy agreement about the dance. I won't fight her about it anymore if she only works the door and doesn't come in to the main part of the gym. I told her I was embarrassed and didn't want her to see me dancing. Like I'll be dancing.

She throws the dress on the bed. "I can't believe how nervous I am. What do you suggest?"

It's good to see her face all lit up, even though waiting for Elliott has etched lines around her eyes. I page through the stuff in her closet. "Do you want tough or sexy?"

"Neither! I'm going with Chuck!"

"Sexy it is. The guy hasn't been out in years. He won't

be hard to please." I pull a black sweater out of the back of her closet. It's soft, like rabbits. I remember this sweater from my Dad days. I hand it to her.

"Oh, no, this old thing?" But she runs it against her cheek.

"Wear it with your black pants, the tight ones. And your silver earrings. Do you need any help with your makeup?"

"No, I think I can do that much myself."

I sit on her bed, watching her get dressed. The pants hug her just right. And the sweater rides only high enough that she won't get thrown out of the dance. She straps on her cell phone.

"You look good, Mom." My voice catches a bit, and she looks at me.

She doesn't say anything, but she comes to the edge of the bed and gives me a hug.

Chuck shows up half an hour early in a billow of cologne and a black turtleneck. It's tucked in, even. His slacks are black wool, with a very nice black belt, and his shoes are shiny black.

"Whoa. Did you max out the old VISA card or what?"

"I needed a few things."

I inspect him from all angles. His hair is curling a little over his ears. He's probably the best-looking troll I've seen.

"You ate something today, did you?"

"Actually yes. A knight going into battle must fortify himself. I had a hunk of red meat and a salad. Super size. And a chocolate shake."

"That about covers the food groups. Let me smell your breath."

He puffs in my face. It smells like toilet bowl cleaner.

"Okay. You pass. So you understand the plan? You are to fight the forces of evil ONLY at the door. DO NOT enter the main gym." I hope Chuck can't hear the real dread in my voice.

"Only the door." He folds me into his arms.

I breathe him in, hating to let him go. Tears threaten to bolt from the corners of my eyes. I wriggle from his embrace, swiping at my eyes. "Get her home by midnight or she turns into a mother."

❖ ❖ ❖

After Mom and Chuck leave, I scrounge something for myself to wear, then make my way over to Ravin's house. When I get there her mother is just leaving, a tennis bag slung over her shoulder. I find Ravin sitting cross-legged on her bed, her eyes closed, headphones over her ears. The volume through the headphones is set to "deafen."

"I'm just going to hide your mom's gun, okay?"

The face remains blank.

"Just in case Mike decides to add it to tonight's entertainment, okay?"

Nothing. Just music.

"Right. Thanks. Nice talking to you."

But when I go into that inner sanctum, that vast-bedded, floral-smelling room, and ease open the drawer with the embroidered hanky, and hold my breath, and slide my hand in, there's only the hanky. The gun is gone.

CHAPTER THIRTY-ONE

—⁓—

I pace on the sidewalk outside of Cor's house, the night cold and the sky so low it drapes me with a dead hand. I don't know if Ravin even knew I'd been there. If she did, she didn't acknowledge me. Now Cor is late. I can hear the sounds of the dance off in the dark: car doors slamming, voices excited, girls laughing.

I go around to the front door and ring the bell. Then I ring it again. After a long time her mother answers. A baby in a sleeper is on her shoulder, making feeble protests. Cor's mother puts her hand to her lips.

I whisper, "Could you tell Cor I'm here. Please."

She shakes her head. "She's sick."

"Again!"

"SSSHH!"

The baby lifts its head and bleats. I get the "now look what you've done" glare from Cor's mother.

I whisper more quietly, "I have to talk to her."

Cor's mother shakes her head. "She's in bed. Asleep. The flu."

Yeah, right.

"Okay. Thanks. Tell her I hope she gets better soon."

Cor's mother is already closing the door on me.

I go round back to Cor's window and tap.

"Let me in. I'm freezing out here."

No answer. I tap a little harder. With my foot. A light comes on in the window above hers.

"This isn't what friends do," I say. "Ditching the other person. Making them go all by themselves to the STUPID dance."

Still nothing. Who said anything about friends?

"Fine. I'm going. I'm not afraid."

The window above me opens and a small round face appears. One of her many siblings.

"My mom says you better clear out or she's going to get her broom."

Your mother is a witch. I kick a clod of dead grass at Cor's window, then I go.

❖ ❖ ❖

There's enough perfume floating around the gym that you can taste it. Slim-shouldered girls in strapped black dresses are leaning on guys in white buttoned shirts and black pants. Mom and Chuck are the door police, checking for bottles. They should be checking for metal.

Ravin finds me. She looks like a chained Doberman.

"Where's Cor?"

"Sick."

She curses softly. "Do you have your hat?"

I pat my bulging pocket. "Yes."

"You have to wear it. The lights are going to go out, and when they do, wherever you are, put on your hat and head for the stage."

"Why are we doing this?"

"If we wear a hat, we help protect the sprayers. Strength in numbers."

"No. I mean, WHY are we doing this? I say we tell someone. Then there won't be a spraying, and we won't have anyone to protect."

Ravin turns to me, her eyes hard. "You stop the action now, then Mike walks away, guaranteed. As I see it, the only way to nail Mike is to let him get caught tonight."

"Mike and how many others?"

"You chose to be here, Marlie. We all did."

"So now you're not afraid of getting caught?"

She shrugs.

A snake of fear coils in my gut. "What do you really have planned?" We all know about the gun: Ravin, me, Cor, Mike. Someone has it.

Ravin ignores my question. "There's no crime in just wearing a hat." She holds up her hand to stop me from saying anything more. "You stay here and watch for Cor. She'll show up. Tell her to wear her hat."

Lex isn't hard to find. He's wearing a white shirt and pants, and his white runners. Only thing is, his underwear isn't white, and it shows like a flag through the pants.

"Hey, Marlie. You look nice."

I didn't do anything with my hair, and I'm wearing a black sweatshirt and jeans. "You are too kind."

He puzzles on that for a while.

"You do, too."

He smiles.

Music is thudding through the wood floor. Mr. Bates is roving, a cell phone up to one ear, a hand clamped over the other against the music, his eyes never leaving the crowd. He sees me, then Lex, and gives us a quick tight smile.

Lex stands with his hands in his pockets, bobbing, his chin jutting in and out half a beat behind the music. His white shirt is pulling a bit across the back.

I wouldn't mind if he asked me to dance.

"I see you brought a friend." Mike's voice is a sneer. Mike is all in black. He's wearing a new jacket, the collar zipped up high around his neck.

Lex stands still, on alert. He takes his hands out of his pockets, slowly.

I move a step away from Lex, distancing him from me.

With the same ugly curl to his mouth, Mike says to Lex, "I need to talk to your DATE. You don't mind, do you?"

Lex blushes red.

"I'm not his date!"

Lex drops his eyes.

"I mean, we didn't come together."

Lex looks at me, then at Mike. Mike is smiling, an unpleasant smile.

"I'll be right back, Lex."

Lex nods, his eyes staying on Mike.

Mike grabs my arm and pulls me to where the others are huddled.

Julian looks up and barely nods. The others don't seem

to notice me. For once, they are quiet. Waiting.

"Everything is set. When the lights go out . . ."

"I know. Ravin already told me. Put the hat on and head for the stage."

"With Cor not here, you'll take a sprayer."

Ravin gasps. "No!" Her eyes are wild. "No, she won't!"

"We're under-powered. She takes a sprayer, or we risk the entire operation."

A ghost of green creeps over Ravin's face.

"This isn't her fight."

"Maybe not. But she's wearing the uniform."

I can hardly make my feet follow Julian as he leads me to a table set up by the stage.

"We shouldn't be doing this, Julian."

"Relax. It's just a joke. People will think it's funny."

"Like the shoplifting was funny?"

His cheeks flush, but he ignores the question. "Put your hand under the table."

I stoop down to look. "Get up!" he hisses. "They're taped under there. You can feel them."

I slide my hand on the underside of the table and feel the lumpy shapes of the sprayers.

"There's not much tape holding them. When you get the signal, give one a good pull and it'll come off. It'll be primed. Just aim it and fire. Aim low. You don't want to get it in anyone's eyes."

"Yeah, right. We wouldn't want anyone to get hurt, would we?"

"Watch you don't get any on your hands. When you're empty, drop your gun and break for the stage door. We'll meet in the hollow at the upper field. Leave your face covered. You'll be invisible in the dark."

"Then what?"

"Then we'll go home. Right on curfew."

He makes it sound so simple. Maybe for him, it is.

"Just one question. What's this really going to accomplish? Do you think this little act of terrorism is actually going to change anything? That by doing it, a halo is going to drop over the school and everyone will practice peace on Earth and goodwill toward men?"

Julian studies me for a minute. "That's more than one question." He puts his hand on my shoulder. I can almost see why Cor likes him. "Use this first sprayer." He shows me with his hand. "There's hardly anything in it. And just aim it at the walls."

Julian leaves me alone to survey the packed gym. There must be a few hundred people just on the dance floor. Keely and Loren have a couple of the senior volleyball players out there. The guys are looking pretty loose. They're waving their arms over their heads and jumping around. Keely and Loren are hardly moving their hips, their hands down at their sides, their eyes flitting to the crowd to see who is watching.

It's just me.

Maybe if I pretend to have the flu, Mom and Chuck will take me home.

"Hey, Marlie." Lex appears at my side. He's holding a can of Coke. He is so white. "Want some? I didn't drink any yet."

"No, thanks."

He tips the can and drinks, the bumpy thing in his throat going up and down as he drains the can. A belch rumbles back out.

"Excuse me."

Where would he get white pants, anyway? Maybe his dad is a painter. I don't like the thought of them covered in red.

"Hey, Lex. You want to walk me home?"

His eyes get round. "Already?" Then he nods yes, really fast.

"Wait for me outside, okay? I've just got a couple of things I've got to do, then I'll be out."

"But if I leave, I can't come back in." He wants to believe me. Wants to believe that I'm not ditching him. Wants to believe that there's a chance that another human being under the age of forty actually cares anything about him.

"Come on, I'll walk you to the door."

His great white shape pauses in the open doorway, and he turns around. Maybe he wants to see if I'm watching him. I am, I guess. But what I'm really watching, behind him, in the black depths of night, is the unmistakable light of falling snow.

It takes everything I've got to turn away from him and go back into the dance.

CHAPTER THIRTY-TWO

━━✍━━

Dance beat is thumping between my ears. I can hear only the bass, like when a car passes you in the street with its stereo full blast. There's no music. Just noise.

The dance floor is jumping now. Everyone's dancing, alone, with partners, in great seething groups. Keely and Loren are dancing. Mike's entire list, except Lex, is dancing. And Cor never came. Only Mike and his army stand on the sidelines, nervous as cats.

Mom and Chuck are leaning on the back wall by the door. Mom is laughing. Chuck is watching the crowd. He sees me and gives a thumbs-up. He's pushed the sleeves of his sweater up his arms. Mom's silver earrings flash splinters of light.

I want Elliott back so bad. Just Elliott.

My hands feel like that woman at the funeral parlor, Ivy — cold, with the weight of the dead. All the strength is gone from me. Mike and Julian are slipping up onto the stage. I pull the hat from my pocket.

Once in my other life, the one with Keely, we were sitting in an assembly, marveling at the painful sounds coming from the Junior Band on stage. Keely was cracking me up, saying the band sounded like a frog in a blender. She was leaning over, talking quietly into my ear, but I laughed out loud. At the very moment the music stopped.

My laughter sounded like a cannon. Kids around me turned to stare, and the teacher shot me a dirty look. Keely looked straight ahead, like she had nothing to do with it. The sound of my laughter just hung there, like something solid. At that moment, it was more real than I was.

Tonight, just before the lights go out, snow is falling outside, Chuck is reaching over to take Mom's hand, and the music stops. And in that tiny moment, all that has gone before doesn't matter anymore. And tomorrow doesn't matter. All I've got is right now.

Then the lights go out.

In the instant of blackness, the gym falls silent. An adult's voice calls out that the breaker for the lights has been disabled. Then people are laughing, cheering the darkness, faceless shapes lit by the dim pools of the exit signs.

The music starts again. It's louder. Insistent. The sound of frenzied feet on the floor pushes me through the dark toward the stage.

Shoulders and hips, even hands press against me as I make my way through the crowd. It's like everyone in the gym is one entity, one huge animal, rolling and stretching, and I'm a bug trying to get out from under it. The smell of it is enormous, animal and perfume, mothballs, liquor, smoke. It's so close I want to gag. I drop the hat.

I'm used to the dark now, and I can see shadowy figures moving on the stage. There's another smell too, a metal smell, but maybe it's my imagination. Maybe I just know it's here. The gun.

Someone pushes past me, the shape familiar even in the dark.

"Cor!"

The figure hesitates, then the crowd swallows it. I push through the crowd after it.

In front of me, someone on the dance floor screams, and I know then that I'm too late. They've started.

"What the . . . ? They've got sprayers!"

At first, the crowd just stands there. But the first round cuts a cold wet swath, and they scream, a few even laugh.

A white-shirted kid near me takes a direct hit, his chest a splatter of red. He stumbles and falls against another guy, and the two of them go down. A girl screams and screams again.

"Shooters!"

The panicked cry is taken up and carried over the crowd.

"Shooters!"

People are on the floor, covered in red, and it looks real. Scary real. And suddenly the animal is a beast, frantic to get out.

Streams of people clamor at the exits. People are screaming. The noise is incredible. They're running, pushing, to find an open exit. Some trip. Others run right over them.

I can hear Ravin, screaming over the crowd, "It's just paint!"

A crowd is starting up the steps to the stage, some to stop the sprayers, but most to find a way out. From the midst of the crowd I see two black-faced sprayers drop their guns and disappear in the crush at the stage door. The floor is covered in paint. People are slipping in it. It's spattered up the walls, even on the ceiling. The gym glows a bizarre red.

Near the main doors, Chuck is on a chair, hollering for people to stop pushing. His hands are held up in front of him, like he's holding back the mob. I can't see my mother. Then Chuck is knocked off his chair. His arms windmill and for an insane minute he's suspended above the crowd, above that crazed and manic beast, and hangs there like a crooked angel. Then he drops.

"Let him up! Let him up!" I'm screaming, running, slipping, getting up, slipping again. "Get off of him!"

I can't get through the crowd. People are piling into me from behind, a wall of backs in front of me. Sometimes, when I fall, hands pick me up. Other times, they step on me.

The breath is ragged in my throat, my thighs are aching with the strain of pushing through the crowd. It's worse at the door, where everyone is piling up. Piling up on Chuck. I thought Chuck and Mom would be safe at the door. I see a shiny black shoe.

I tear at people's backs, pulling hair and collars and whatever I can grab to free Chuck from the crush. I can see him now. He's on his belly. His eyes are closed. I attack the mob, prying people off of him.

"You're going to kill him!" I'm sobbing now, paint and tears and snot all over my face. There are too many. I can't do it anymore. My voice is gone. My arms and legs and back just give up. I slump into a heap beside Chuck, and take his hand. It feels cold. My voice isn't anything now, just a whisper.

"You're going to kill him."

Huge white hands reach down in front of me and toss crazed people like feed sacks. It's Lex, heaving people off the pile, swinging them clear, then bending for another and another. Most find their feet and join the crush at the door. Some sink down beside me, sucking air in whooping gulps, just glad to be free of the pile.

"Chuck!" His body is all twisted up and something red is trickling out of his nose. I have an awful feeling it's not paint.

Feet thud into my back and come down on Chuck.

"You've got to get up!"

His body jolts as feet vault off of him. They're even stepping on his face.

"I've got him!" Lex crosses Chuck's chest with one massive arm and begins dragging him toward the door. Then he reaches his other hand down for me.

"Come on, Marlie. You're almost there."

I look up at him, and his pink face is shining with the strain of holding Chuck. His eyes are pleading. "Come on."

I reach my hand up, and I feel his, the power in it, the absolute hugeness, as his fingers close on mine.

I don't even know why I look behind me. Maybe it's his voice, not a scared voice, but angry, cursing. Mike. He's not wearing his mask. He's tangled in the crowd, his fists and elbows flying as he fights. Nice of him to stick around. Clearly, he never took a sprayer. Still, I'm glad this thing is over.

The crowd surges and I feel Lex's arm pull tight.

Mike is further back now. He plows into a guy, forcing himself around him. He's forcing himself away from the door.

181

No. No, no no! Mike wasn't trying to get out. He was trying to stay in.

His back is to me now, and he's free of the crowd. He's running, and I'm losing him in the dark. But I see him put on the balaclava.

I'm struggling to get to my feet, but there are people between Lex and me now. My hands are bloody from Chuck and covered in paint, and they slip. I feel Lex grab, but our hands slip apart.

"Marlie!" he screams.

"I'm all right." There must be twenty people now between us. As they push forward, I let them elbow me aside, out of their way. I don't know if Lex can even hear me. "Just get Chuck out."

His white head disappears. I can hear Lex, his voice thundering, "Marlie!"

I could follow him, just slip into his broad white wake and be out of the gym. Be out of it all. At the fringe of the mob now, I turn back for the stage. I've got to find Mike.

CHAPTER THIRTY-THREE

—ᵐᵐ—

On the steps to the stage I practically crash into Ravin. Her pants are covered in paint. She sees me, and her eyes widen in the balaclava.

I yank the hat off her head. "Where's Mike?"

Her eyes dart over the crowd. "I lost him. There are so many people."

The main exit is still jammed. More people are pushing their way onto the stage, their feet thundering on the wooden stairs as they rush the stage door. A few students are huddled on the dance floor, some in splayed heaps, crying. A hooded figure at the bottom of the stage stairs is pumping a paint gun at the pileup by the door. I see a couple of spray guns dropped on the floor. I can hear sirens. Dance music is thumping, frantic, like it's measuring the heartbeat of the crowd.

Each time someone slips, the screams start up again. "Shooters!"

I scan the stage. "He's not done yet." In case you were thinking of leaving.

Ravin's voice is small, frightened. She grips my arm.

"He might have a gun. My mother's gun."

"I know."

So Ravin looked for the gun too. But she doesn't have it.

"Wait for the cops," she says. "We don't have to do this."

I push her hand away. "If Mike has the gun, then he's going to shoot someone. And we don't get to pick. Would you rather it be your dad?"

Ravin clasps her arms. She shakes her head no. Then an older guy twice her size shoves her out of his way as he runs for the stage door. She sprawls on the floor.

That's when I see him, hunched in a corner of the stage, his Velcro shoes, his black jacket unzipped to reveal a bright white T-shirt.

"There he is." I nudge Ravin with my foot and indicate with my head where I've found him.

Mike's hands are resting on a guitar case. He's fumbling with the clasps. He looks up, as if he's heard me, but he doesn't seem to see me. Beneath the balaclava his eyes are round. One of his friends is with him, the kid's eyes crazed with panic. The kid is clenching a guitar case to his chest.

Guitars? What are they doing with guitars?

The sirens are close now. Really close.

Mike must hear them too. He curses, says something to the kid and jerks his thumb toward the door. The kid yanks off his balaclava and, still carrying the guitar case, bolts to the stage door.

Mike takes his hat off too. He makes a move to get up, but then freezes. His face turns stone gray, his lips are moving, as if in silent prayer. I follow his stare.

Just off to our side, on the stage, a slim figure in a lacy

top is leveling a handgun at his head.

"Cor." Her name escapes me in a sigh.

In her own way, Cor's been talking for weeks about doing this. About sacrifice. And protecting the all at the expense of the one. About there being no such thing as an innocent bystander. She's using two hands on the gun, and it's shaking.

Ravin is struggling to get to her feet. "It's my mother's gun!"

Mike's hands drop to his sides. His chest is barely moving. His voice quakes. "Cor, put it down, okay?" He's shrinking, deflating like an old balloon.

Cor's arms straighten toward him, the gun bobbing crazily in her hands. It's like she can barely handle the weight. When she speaks, it's as if she's talking to herself.

"This is for what you did to me. You said it was them, but it was you. Maybe no one else knows what you did. But I do. I have always known, even if I didn't want to admit it. And now I have my chance to make things right."

"You better put that away," he says. "Before the cops get here."

In the smallest motion, she shakes her head. Maybe I wasn't really scared before, when she was just Cor, holding a gun, aiming it, shaking like a normal person. Because then, in the next instant, a calm comes over her, a horrible resolve, and her hands are firm on the weapon, absolutely sure. Now I'm scared.

Part of me wants her to do it, just blast Mike out of our lives. But not Cor. I don't want her paying for all of us. Not anymore. When I look at Mike, his menace is gone and all I see is a frightened kid.

"Cor!" It's my dream scream, and no sound comes out.

But I hear her name, called from the guy with the sprayer. He's looking at her, tiny white movements around his eyes like butterflies. It's Julian.

"NO!" Julian spins around to face her. "Don't do it!"

Sirens are drilling into the gym from all sides. She's run out of time. She must realize that. But she's still aiming the gun.

Ravin's voice reaches me from the floor. "If she shoots, she could do adult time."

Cor's chest lifts as she takes a steadying breath. Her hands tense on the gun. If she's heard Julian, I can't tell. No one else seems to exist for her except Mike. She's deadly calm now, and I swear I can see her finger closing over the trigger.

A stream of red hits Cor in the face. Julian is pumping the last of the paint right at her eyes.

I hear Cor gasp, then choke, then suck a breath. She screams. Her hands come up to her face. The gun falls. She claws at her eyes, trying to clear the paint.

Ravin vaults for the gun.

"My eyes! I can't see!"

I throw myself against Cor, knocking her to the floor. Her eyes are two red balls, running red into her nose and mouth. Bubbles of red break under her nostrils as she sucks for air.

Ravin rolls in next to me. In one smooth motion she gathers the handgun and buries it in her clothing. Then she screams in my ear, "Shooters!"

Mike is running now, holding the guitar case against his chest, battering his way through the crush of people, fleeing toward the stage door.

A guitar case. It's a guitar case. Not a guitar. He's got something in that case, something he doesn't want to leave behind. Julian's words echo my worst fears, "That little bitty thing?"

I scramble for footing, trying to get up, trying to stop him.

Ravin pulls me back down, slamming my head to the floor.

Heavy blue suits materialize around the perimeter of the gym, armed with rifles and vests. "Get down on the floor! Hands out to the side!"

I can hear Julian. He's crying. "Please don't shoot."

Cor is sobbing, a high-pitched wail of pain and loss.

Ravin is still screaming. "Shooters!"

I scream too, "He's got a gun! Stop him!"

An officer kneels down next to us.

Mike slips through the stage door.

"A gun!" I point at the door.

The officer rests a hand on my shoulder. "You're safe now girls." His flashlight arcs around the gym as he takes in the wreckage. He shakes his head. "It's just paint."

❧ ❧ ❧

The ambulance's doors slam shut and it whoops a warning siren to clear the throng before barreling off into the night. Cor is in there, her eyes bandaged, her hands tied to her sides so she can't tear at the dressing. All over the street, people are standing, shivering, some holding on to each other, others in speechless silence, some laughing the crazy laugh of people just off a roller coaster. Spokes of red and blue police lights slash across pale faces.

Snow is falling. It's coming down in huge flakes, capping everyone in brilliant white. A group of guys in paint-stained clothes pelt snowballs at one another. I spot Keely to one side, crying and hanging on Loren.

Harried police officers with notebooks collect reports. In the back of a police car, Julian sits with his head lowered.

A brown-suited man pushes his way through the uniforms.

"Ravin. Thank God you're all right." He wraps Ravin with his arms, presses her against him, and holds her. His eyes fill and she starts to sob.

"Come on," he says to Ravin. "I'll take you home."

He leads her through the crowd, his arm massive on her thin shoulders. Her hand clutches the back of his suit jacket.

She got the gun. She'll put it back. No one will ever know.

More ambulances are leaving, loaded with people hurt in the panic. I suppose Chuck is in one of them. I haven't been able to find him or Mom.

I'm tired all of a sudden, so tired my legs feel like they might collapse. I have to find out about Chuck.

I don't care if we all get caught. In a way, it would be a relief.

What's bigger is what didn't happen — what Mike didn't do. What Cor tried to do.

Then I see Mom. She's standing by a police car, a frantic look on her face, snow lacing her sweater like a shawl. She sees me and her face crinkles up and she starts to cry.

She cries a keening sound, her shoulders heaving and the tears streaming down her face. I go to her and she pulls me to her.

"I'm right here, Mom." Then I lie, "Everything's okay."

CHAPTER THIRTY-FOUR

~~~

The snow this morning comes up to my knees, bone dry. It sifts over my feet in a *shush shush* noise as I push through it. McLean is on his driveway, hauling out his sled from the open garage. He looks up as I pass, but he doesn't say anything. He's intent on the sled.

Keely's curtains are still closed.

Ravin's voice comes to mind: "Some people like dangerous friends. It makes them feel powerful." Keely likes Loren. She used to like me.

Mom and I went straight to the hospital last night to see Chuck. He was unconscious, plugged with tubes up his nose and down his throat, and he was the sickest shade of gray I've ever seen.

Mom settled into a chair next to him and held his hand. She talked to him through the night, quiet things and things I didn't know.

I wandered through the emergency ward, stepping over paint-spattered kids who were waiting to get stitched up, their parents' faces sometimes angry, sometimes almost blank with the horror of what might have been. All of them were in pain. I found Lex, sitting all by himself, an orange Popsicle in his hand. He smiled when he saw me.

"Are you hurt?" I searched his big pink face for signs of injury.

"No."

I breathed a sigh of relief. "You probably saved Chuck's life. I didn't know you were still at the dance. I thought you'd already left."

"I was waiting for you."

"Oh, Lex. I'm sorry. I didn't want you there. I didn't want you in that."

He was looking at his knees, but he nodded.

"So what are you doing here at the hospital?"

"Waiting for you. Again." He looked up finally. "They're giving out Popsicles. Do you want one?"

I heard a commercial once for the lottery. It said, "This could change your life." And I got to thinking, a lot of things change your life. Every day. Small decisions and mistakes, the wrong word at the wrong time.

Red paint.

My father.

My father will never see that what he did is wrong. But that doesn't make it right. And he'll never admit that taking Elliott changed my life. But it did. I'm not blaming everything on my father. Maybe I would have got sucked into Mike's madness anyway. But I'm not sucked in anymore.

I took a Popsicle from Lex. "My mom is going to stay here with Chuck. Would you walk me home now?"

And he did.

The morning air is so cold it makes my eyes water. The

snow has stopped. It covers the school fields in pure white light. It's like last night didn't even happen.

Ravin answers the door in her pajamas. Yellow pajamas, with little white rabbits.

"I used to have some of those," I say. In fifth grade. Her face is scrubbed clean of makeup and paint. She looks fragile. Normal. I'd almost expect to hear the sound of Saturday morning cartoons.

I follow her into the kitchen. She pours me an enormous bowl of Frosted Flakes and shoves the milk jug to me.

We sit side by side and eat, reading the back of the cereal box.

"Dad says Julian is taking full responsibility." Her spoon is going up and down, the tattoo like a kite. "And that some of the parents want blood."

"I bet."

"Cor can't see anything yet."

The cereal stops in my throat. I nod, but I can't speak. Tears are dripping into my bowl.

She lays her small white hand on my arm. "I have to change schools. My parents' decision. They say James Last is too rough. They're getting me into St. Margaret's after the break. Pulling some strings. They won't even let me finish the semester at James Last."

I look at her, so much like a kid in those pajamas. Maybe at St. Margaret's we could have become real friends. "Well," I say, trying to swallow my tears. "You're going to look hot in that blue plaid uniform."

She's holding her head in her hands.

"Oh, come on," I say. "It won't be that bad. You'll get used to the knee socks. And that cute little tie."

She looks up, and the tears in those white-blue eyes makes them almost transparent. "I'm serious, Marlie. Mike didn't finish anything last night."

I tell her my suspicion about what was in the guitar cases.

She drops her eyes. "There was some talk about big weapons."

I let my spoon clatter in my bowl. "And you didn't tell anyone?"

"It was a long time ago and anyway, it was just talk."

"But then you went to get your mom's gun. You knew what he was going to do."

"No. I only knew that I was scared, and my mom's gun was gone, and I thought he must have taken it."

"Why did you put on the mask?"

She bats her hand at the question. "I saw you at the door, I saw Lex helping you. I thought you were out. I didn't think Cor was there at all. I lost Mike in all the mayhem. So I put on the mask. As much as I didn't want to, I thought I might be a little safer."

"From Mike? I'm not sure that would have made any difference. Nevkeet wouldn't think so. And neither would Cor, it sounds like."

"Cor," she says, and one eyebrow lifts. "You notice she didn't wear a mask?"

Ravin's tone makes me bristle. "She's not afraid anymore. She's not part of Mike's insanity. She's broken free."

"Maybe," Ravin says. "Or else she doesn't care anymore, and didn't plan on leaving that gym alive. Good thing for Cor that Julian saw her."

What she says settles over me in the chilly stillness of the kitchen.

"God. Julian." When he sprayed Cor, he was stopping her from killing herself. If he knew about those guitar cases, would he still have stopped her? I feel like I'm betraying Cor for even thinking it, but I don't think he would have. Even if it meant losing Cor, he would have chosen to stop Mike. "He couldn't have known Mike's real plan."

"Plan?" Ravin leans back in her chair and crosses her arms. "You don't know what was in those guitar cases, if anything. I would have heard if there was."

"Like you heard about the shoplifting?" I shake my head. "No, Ravin. I'm not wrong about this."

Ravin shrugs, but she's not convincing me. She's scared too. "Well," she says. "I guess you're going to have to be careful, then. And Cor too. At least I'll be in a different school."

Careful.

Chuck says that, too, when we play chess. Don't be reckless. Be careful. But sometimes, with the Queen, the board calls for drastic moves. Sometimes, the whole game depends on her blind, courageous action. She alone has the power and mobility. She alone can change the course of a match, with just one move.

In my mind I don her crown and sword. My Queen is anything but careful.

Nana's voice comes over the intercom sounding gravelly and weak. "I'm sick in bed, Marlena. I have the most terrible cold. You'll have to come up another time."

"But I've brought a Christmas present for Prancey." I clasp a plush bear that I doubt will last longer than two sessions with that little beast.

There's a long silence, then her voice returns, sounding softer. "A gift for Prancey. Won't he be pleased. You can leave it outside my door." The buzzer sounds, letting me in.

I'd wanted to see Nana, to study her for signs that Dad had called. With a sigh I punch the elevator button to take me up.

When the elevator opens I'm surprised to see a package already by Nana's door. On it is a sheet of paper with Nana's careful printing: "For pick-up by ABC Couriers."

I plunk the bear down beside it. If Nana doesn't retrieve it before the courier comes, it might get picked up, too. I move the sign a little farther over onto the package, and give the bear a pat on the head. "Good luck. You'll need it."

Then a familiar shape catches my eye under the sheet of paper. I lift Nana's sign. The package is wrapped with brown paper and tied with string. In the same neat printing, Nana has addressed it and added, "Hold for pick-up by receiver on December 23." A week from now. Tucked under the string is a smaller parcel. It's the book I left for Elliott.

One week. Seven days. One hundred sixty-eight hours. Nana surely meant for me to see that courier package. I hereby vow to be a much better granddaughter. Maybe I'll bake her some cookies, something healthy, with wheat germs, or whatever that stuff is called.

CHAPTER THIRTY-FIVE

~~~

Monday morning, and no one is in a hurry to go into class. Everyone is talking about the dance, about Julian, talking about what the newspapers said. I'm trying to be invisible.

"Too bad about Cor." Mike's voice behind me in the crowded corridor makes me spin. He's walking alone, his eyes elsewhere in the crowd, as if he's talking to himself. But he's talking to me. I turn away, and walk faster.

"I hear she's going to get a seeing eye dog. She should get something that suits her, something like a pitbull bitch."

I'm trying to ignore him, but my skin is crawling.

"Quite the solo act she performed on the stage. Wonder how long before Julian sings?"

This makes me stop, and he actually walks into me. He's so close I can see the hole above his eyebrow and its thin covering of skin. He stinks of breath and ointment.

"What Julian did was out of honor," I hiss. "Out of something real between him and Cor."

He snorts and droplets of spit hit my face. "He did it to

protect me. And because Cor deserved it."

"Like he did what he was told? Not this time, Mike. If he didn't know before, he knows now. You set him up to cover for you. You set us all up. But now he's ditched you. We all have, even your guitar-playing goon."

He grabs the front of my jacket. His eyes are bulging and his lips have disappeared in an angry line. "That dance was just a rehearsal. I'd be real happy to include you and your mom in the next performance. Give the gravedigger some family business. You don't know anything about anything. Remember that." Then he shoves me, hard, and I'm on my butt in the middle of the hall floor.

"Hey!" some guy yells. Mike doesn't even look over his shoulder, just flips him the finger and disappears in the crowd.

The guy helps me to my feet. "Are you okay?"

I brush off the seat of my pants, my face bright red, my eyes threatening to spill. Then an image comes to me of Annie, Annie in her dull green burial dress. Annie who couldn't tell. Not this time, Annie. "Yeah," I say. "Thanks. I'll be fine."

❧ ❧ ❧

Two bouquets of flowers, one from the school, the other from Ravin, sit on the table by Cor's bed. I might have brought her some too, except I came from school. Not that Cor can see the flowers. And if there's any scent, it disappears in the smells of Monday lunch. Cor's tray is opened, untouched, beside her. She is bandaged, lying limp on the sheets, only the warmth in her hand saying she's not dead.

"They treat me like I'm some kind of hero, everyone around here. Like Julian is evil and I'm not." Her voice is so flat it scares me.

I glance at the door. Staff are bustling back and forth in the hallway, but we're as alone as we can be in a hospital.

"I'm sorry, Cor."

She turns to me, her eyes a white padded helmet.

"They say, 'You should be bouncing back now. It's all behind you.' I say, let me curl up and die."

"No, Cor, please don't talk like that."

"Forget about it. Go away. Leave me alone." She turns her head away from me, her hand completely without life.

I squeeze it, hard. "It was Mike that beat you up last year, wasn't it?"

She pulls her hand away from me.

"What are you afraid of, Cor? Look at you. What more can he do?"

Her voice is cold and dark and like a knife in my guts. "You just have no idea."

The memory of this morning with Mike comes over me like dampness, and I shudder. "You have to tell someone, Cor."

"He'll tell them that I had a gun. That I should go to jail just like Julian. And won't that look good on my scholarship application?"

"You didn't tell Julian that it was Mike who hurt Nevkeet, did you?"

She's so still it's like the voice is coming from somewhere else.

"No. I didn't want to believe it myself."

A long sigh shudders from her.

"It doesn't matter, what he did to me. I didn't see him. We were walking home from the mall. I was giving him a hard time. He'd told me he set a house on fire, one of the new ones being built in his neighborhood. He was bragging. He said he wanted to set his mom's house on fire next. I told him he was an idiot. That he had to get some help. We argued for a while. Then he said that I was right. If I didn't tell anyone about the fire, he wouldn't set any more. But his face was weird, like all his feelings had gone deep underground. I turned to go home. And that's all I really remember."

"There was no one else around? No one who might have seen something?"

"I don't know. I'm tired, Marlie. I'm just so tired."

I want to shake her, shake some life into her voice.

"He's planning something, Cor. He's going to do something that makes the dance look like a Girl Guide meeting. And I'm not going to let it happen." I push the chair away from the bed and stand up.

At the door, her voice stops me. "What are you going to do?"

I answer her without turning around. "I don't know yet. Maybe I'm going to fight fire with fire."

She's quiet again, so I start to leave.

"Hey, Marl."

I stop.

"They say this blindness is just temporary."

I breathe, and it feels like I haven't breathed in days, and the hospital air is the sweetest I've ever tasted.

"That's a good thing, Cor." I glance back at her, lying there, her face to the ceiling, her arms straight down by her sides. "I'm leaving now."

No response.

"Bye."

She doesn't say anything. I pause at the doorway, then join the busy stream of people in the hall, letting it carry me away from her room.

CHAPTER THIRTY-SIX

On Tuesday, Mr. Bates had me in his office for over an hour. He asked me about Julian, how well I knew him, if I thought he had planned this to get back at Cor for breaking up with him. I was glad I could tell him some good things about Julian. Mr. Bates asked me if I wore one of the balaclavas. When I said no, he carefully avoided asking me anything more.

Ms. Grimshaw found me in the hall later that afternoon and gave me a hug. "I'm sorry about your friend. I hope you're all right."

People are still eyeing each other warily in the corridors. Everyone knows Julian and Mike were friends. But Mike came out of his interrogation by the principal totally clean. Some people still suspect him, but no one is sure who was involved. Stories are racketing back and forth about all kinds of students with vendettas. They even have Julian working for a rival school.

Lex and I are leaning on the bike stand after school on Wednesday, the one with Julian's bike still chained up. I don't tell him it was Julian's. That's between me and Cor.

He doesn't seem to think it's weird that there's a bike in the stand.

I say to him, "How much do you know about Mike?"

He's wearing a knitted headband from the gas bar on the corner, the kind you get free when you fill your tank. He scratches at it.

"You mean stuff I've heard?"

"I mean stuff you really know."

He shrugs and looks down at his feet. "I've seen him cut tires. I told you about that. But I guess you're asking because of what happened at the dance."

I nod, avoiding his eyes.

"Well, I didn't see him do anything, not at the dance. And I didn't see you doing anything, either. Except helping your friend Chuck."

I smile at him gratefully.

"But he could get you into trouble, couldn't he?" he says.

"I am in trouble, Lex, whether or not anyone finds out. I didn't stop him."

Lex jams the toe of his boot into the snow, making a crescent-shaped furrow. "I've seen him do something else."

I wait for him to continue, watching his face.

"I didn't stop him, either."

His big boot is pushing the snow back and forth.

I hesitate, choosing my words. "That day at my locker, when you saw Cor, your face changed. You looked sick, all of a sudden. And what you said about Mike, about him beating up people . . ." I draw in my breath.

His eyes fill.

"I can't do this by myself, Lex. I need your help."

With a quavering voice, he says, "This guy was kicking

her and she was just lying there. I didn't try to help her. Each time he kicked her, her body kind of lifted up. I told myself that I wasn't really seeing it, that it couldn't be happening. And I just ran away. I didn't even have the guts to call the cops."

I try to contain all that I'm feeling. "You saw him, right? You saw Mike beating Cor?"

"It was getting dark. I'd seen them a few minutes earlier, walking. They cut through the hollow on the top field. I stayed on the sidewalk. When I got to the corner I looked back, and I could just make it out, what he was doing. I know it was him. But I didn't really see him."

I know it was Mike, too. But it's not enough.

I tell Lex about the smoke bomb at the school office and how Mrs. Birk didn't believe me. I tell him about Nevkeet and what Cor told me about the house fire. Then I say, "You could do something now."

He wipes at his eyes with his glove. His eyes are so pink. He nods and puts my arm through his and sighs.

☆ ☆ ☆

Chuck is out of the hospital, although his head is still bandaged where they stitched him up. He's sitting in our living room, under a blanket on the couch. I'm in the kitchen with Mom, peeling carrots for supper.

"Elaine next door seems to think you might know the boy who was caught at the dance. She says he's part of some group at your school."

The only sound I make is the *scrape scrape* of my peeler.

"Are you part of that group?"

I could deny it, but that doesn't seem fair to Julian. I sidestep. "He's not a bad kid, Julian. I think he got caught up in something that went wrong. I'm sure he never meant for anyone to get hurt."

Scrape scrape.

"You didn't answer me." She grabs the carrot from my hand and bangs it on the counter.

Her eyes are wide-open scared.

"What do you want me to tell you, Mom? That I'm a terrorist? That I let you stand at the door of that dance, let Chuck get almost killed by a stampede of people?"

She takes me by the hands. Hers are ice-cold. "You're not a bad kid, either. It could have been you in the police car. Elliott gone, and you too . . ."

"But it wasn't. And it won't be."

She squeezes my hands. "You've been so alone."

We all have been, Mom, I think, but say instead, "Maybe things will get better now."

"Like Elliott will come back?"

"It could happen." I wish I could tell you.

She shakes her head at me. "Stay away from those people at school. I need to know that you're safe."

"I will, Mom." After tonight.

She looks at me like it's the first time she's seen me.

"You're different now, somehow. You seem so sure of yourself." She reaches up and strokes my hair. "I know you're not telling me everything."

"You mean my hair color? 'Mahogany Sunset.' This time I used the color tube."

"I'm not joking."

But she smiles a little.

"Now we better feed Chuck," I say. "We don't want him to expire on the couch."

Mom takes the scraped carrot, cuts it into sticks, plunks them on a plate, and hands it to me. "I'm more worried about you right now than Chuck. But go ahead and give him these."

And it could happen that Mom and Chuck might live happily ever after.

I take Chuck the carrot sticks and sit with him on the couch. I wish I felt as sure as Mom seems to think I do. I just have to get through tonight, then the rest of the week. Then, maybe, I can ditch this chess queen routine.

"Mom is making you pot roast." The kitchen is clattering with the sounds of her efforts. "With garlic mashed potatoes."

"Ooh." Chuck gazes with rapture at the kitchen door.

"When you've got your strength back, there's a little errand we need to run."

"Sure. Whatever you like." He's fixed on the kitchen door, like that's going to somehow speed up dinner.

"A little road trip." Like a three-hour drive into the bald winter prairie to a town that's barely a dot on the map, where a package is waiting. Oh God, I hope it's still waiting there.

Reluctantly, he pulls his eyes back to mine.

"What are you talking about?"

"You'll see." In about a million seconds. My hands suddenly feel sweaty, and I busy myself, tucking the blanket in around his legs. "Oh, and apple pie. Mom made you apple pie."

His eyes return to the kitchen door. "Apple pie. Did she

make the crust herself?"

"Of course she did. Mom's no slouch in the kitchen. When she wants to, she can cook a mean meal."

"I think I'm in love."

CHAPTER THIRTY-SEVEN

~~~

I set my alarm so that I would be sure to wake up, but I didn't need to. I must have watched every minute click past. Finally, I swing my legs out of bed and get dressed. As I creep past Mom's door, I can hear her snoring softly. In the kitchen, the dishes from our supper are stacked on the drying rack. It still smells like pot roast. I slip out the back door into the night.

Lex is waiting for me at the bike rack at the school.

"Did anyone see you?"

He shakes his head.

"Any sign of Ravin?"

"No."

I stifle my disappointment. When I told her about it she said it was a crazy stunt and we'd get ourselves caught for sure.

Camouflaging Lex for a night raid is a little like disguising a polar bear. I pull a knitted hat over his white hair, and smear eyebrow pencil on his cheeks to darken the dinner plate shine of his face. His tiny eyes are bright with fear.

"You have the flashlight, right?"

He nods.

"If anything happens, if we get separated, then the other person goes ahead with it. Right?"

He nods.

"This is a good thing we're doing."

He nods.

"Then let's go."

The night air is brittle and the lane dark. We trot in silence, our breath in clouds. Bare-limbed trees and back fences are our only witnesses — even dogs are inside on a night like this.

At Mike's street we turn onto the sidewalk. I pull the hat down farther over my face and motion to Lex to pull his down, too. We walk purposefully, like we do this every night at 2:00.

At Mike's, Lex reaches the key down from its spot above the garage side door. I can't see in the dark, but I bet it's been outlined in Magic Marker. My breath is short and ragged. I close the garage door behind us.

It's pitch black. Lex takes a small flashlight from his pocket and shines it on the boxes on the shelves.

"He must keep his stuff in here, the stuff for the smoke bombs. Maybe the fire, too. Look for a box labeled 'Mike'," I whisper.

Lex rolls his eyes and searches the shelves.

At the back of the workbench, behind others marked "Belt Sander" and "Spare Weed Whacker Cord," is a long box with nothing on the side.

"Try that one."

Lex reaches in and hefts the box out onto the floor.

There's a pair of black coveralls on the top, like the ones they wear in shop class. The shoulder crest says "Mike." My palms are sweating in my gloves.

Carefully, I move the coveralls out of the way.

"This is it!" Lex says. "It's just like the picture on the Web site."

I hand Lex the smoke bomb from the top of the box.

"Shine the light down into the box."

Gingerly, I pull aside pieces of pipe and wire. Then I gasp.

"No," Lex whispers but it echoes in the garage.

At the bottom of the box, lying in crumpled newspaper, is a box of ammunition. Big shells. For a really big gun.

"Leave it out," he says, pointing to the box. "They'll find it when they check out the smoke alarm."

I nod, my chest closing on each breath.

Lex is inspecting the smoke bomb, puzzling out where to attach the fuse.

"It isn't long enough. We won't have time to get away."

"Can't you make it longer?"

"There's no more fuse. I looked."

My heart sinks. Lex had come up with the plan. If we could find the smoke bomb and set it off in Mike's garage, the police would investigate and discover it was like the one used at the school. It wasn't much, but it might be enough to get him expelled. Now, though, knowing about the ammunition, it was our only hope to stop him. "Set it up," I hiss at Lex. "Then you go. I'll light it. I don't care if I get caught."

"No. We can come back another time. I'll get some more fuse."

"It's got to be tonight, Lex. He could move that box or get rid of it."

He looks at me, his smudged face ridiculous but so innocent. "I won't leave you here."

Maybe it's because I'm thinking about Lex, that his eyes aren't so small, really, and that he has a nice smile, that I don't notice the garage door open. But I hear it close. Someone has come in.

A flashlight beam blinds me, then I hear Ravin's voice.

"My dad came in late. I had to wait until he fell asleep."

My heart is thumping against my jacket, and my throat is stuck together. All I can do is stare dumbly.

"Did I scare you? Sorry."

I just shake my head and try to get control of my tongue.

She kneels down beside Lex and looks in the box, swearing softly.

Lex is setting the fuse. "There's only like two minutes of fuse," he tells her. "It's not enough time."

"Two minutes is more than enough. For me." She takes the matches from his hand. "You and Marlie go home. I'll light this and be long gone before it goes off."

I saw Ravin run the day Nevkeet was hurt, and I know she's right. I nod to Lex.

Trust your instincts. Do the right thing. Okay, Mom, I hear you. Just as soon as we get Elliott back.

My feet are ice-cold in my bed when I hear the distant sirens.

CHAPTER THIRTY-EIGHT

—— ~~~ ——

"You're going to have to park in beside the building. This car is a dead giveaway." I yawn and stretch. We've driven since long before dawn to get here before the courier office opens. It was tough to convince Chuck that we shouldn't tell Mom. But he wants Dad to turn himself in, and anyway, what if Dad and Elliott don't show up? Why break Mom's heart again? Mom thinks I'm going snowboarding with Ravin's family. I don't know what Chuck told her, if anything. He said he'd never lie to her. His doctor has given him the "all clear," and he says he feels great. I know he's never looked happier.

Chuck pulls the car to the side of the parking lot and backs it in by the office, so we can see the entrance.

"I can't believe your grandmother actually told you she was sending a parcel to your father."

"She didn't. Not exactly. I mean, she didn't use his name on it. But I know it was for him."

"So now we wait."

"Yup. For as long as it takes."

The thought did occur to me that Elliott might not want

to leave Dad. And I wouldn't blame him. But I'm trusting Dad to do the right thing. I think he will. Nana did.

Chuck hands me a carrot stick from a bag beside him. "Your friend out of the hospital yet?"

"Yeah. She has to stay out of the bright light for a while, but she's okay."

"Nice she's home before Christmas."

"Uh-huh."

I crunch the carrot to bits.

"So, are you going to take Mom on a real date?"

"What is a real date, anyway?"

I take another carrot stick and wave it like a conductor's baton. "Flowers, then a nice meal somewhere with real tablecloths, some wine maybe, then, the all-important good-night kiss."

"You've thought this out."

"Well, up to the part about the kiss. You can figure that out for yourself."

He smiles and I can tell he's already thought about it.

"I'm not sure your mother's ready for a relationship."

I shake the carrot at him. "Of course she is. Just go slow."

He nods his head. "I'll give your mother all the time she needs."

"She really likes you." I check his face. "Are you blushing?"

He doesn't answer, but whatever it is, it looks good on him.

We both sit silently, watching the empty parking lot. I think back over the last days of school.

Mr. Bates had half the students in tears at the assembly just before school let out for the holidays. He spoke about tolerance. And forgiveness. Maybe Ms. Grimshaw lent him her book.

Maybe it was the season, because people seemed to hear Mr. Bates. Maybe it was because Mike's been caught for setting the smoke bomb, and now the police are asking him hard questions about the dance, and why he had ammunition in his possession. His name is never used in the newspaper, but I know it's Mike.

Maybe Mike will keep quiet about the rest of us. Maybe not.

❖ ❖ ❖

I must have fallen asleep, because Chuck is jabbing me in the side. It's snowing, and the late morning light is flat and colorless. I rub my eyes, trying to clear the sleep.

"Merry Christmas," he says.

Dad's car is pulling into the lot.

Suddenly I'm afraid. What if he sees us? What if Elliott isn't in the car?

Chuck gives me a reassuring nod. "Go get your brother."

The wind is cold and I shiver in my jacket. As I come around the corner of the building, Dad is climbing out of his car.

He glances around the lot. He looks thin — and gray. Pain stabs at my heart.

Then I see a small head bobbing in the back seat, and a face appears at the window.

I whisper, "Elliott."

Dad takes a step from the car, then stops. He looks right at me.

First he smiles, like he's happy to see me. Then he turns ashen. I see him mouth my name. He looks up at the sky, then back to me, something like apology in his eyes, then he hangs his head.

Goodbye Dad.

The back door of the car opens and Elliott bursts out. He's running toward me, his face beaming. His jacket is flapping undone and he's stumbling in the snow, laughing, getting up, running toward me and calling my name.

I crumple to my knees, laughing now too, and fling open my arms to catch him.

Elliott is coming home.